THE MILLIONAIRE PLAN

KAREN KING

© 2016 Karen King

The right of Karen King to be identified as the author of this work has been asserted by her in accordance with the Copyright, Designs and Patents Act 1988.

The story contained within this book is a work of fiction. Names and characters are the product of the author's imagination and any resemblance to actual persons, living or dead, is entirely coincidental.

All rights reserved. No part of this book may be reproduced, stored in a retrieval system, or transmitted in any form or by any means, electronic, electrostatic, magnetic tape, mechanical, photocopying, recording or otherwise, without the written permission of the copyright holder.

Published by Accent Press Ltd 2016

Paperback ISBN: 9781786154408

Chapter One

Rule number 1: Make sure you're seen at the right places

Great. Here she was, dressed to kill and without a clue what to do, Amber thought, tugging self-consciously at the hem of her dress. Everyone else was walking around in groups, or at least in pairs, chatting and laughing together and making her wish that she'd taken up Callie's offer to go sailing with her and Simon instead of wandering around Coombe Bay Marina alone. Honestly, dressed in this skin-tight, short white designer dress, high heels, and the pile of make-up Callie had insisted she wore, she might as well have the words 'gold-digger' written on her forehead.

Well, that's what she was, wasn't it?

Not for the first time she wondered how she'd let Callie talk her into coming here to try and hook a millionaire. It was mad. Insane. Immoral.

And her only option if she didn't want her parents to lose their home as well as their business.

Spotting a café overlooking the marina, she bought herself a latté and was making her way over to one of the tables when a white yacht caught her eye. It wasn't huge or brash, like some of the yachts in the marina, but it was definitely classy. The sort that a millionaire would have for his own use, to sail around in rather than show off and entertain his friends. As she peered over at it, trying to read the name painted on the side, she collided into something hard. Her coffee cup went flying off the saucer, emptying its contents over a pair of cut-off denim shorts that were hugging lean, definitely male, hips.

'Whoa!' Strong, suntanned arms held her steady. 'You want to try looking where you're going,' an incredibly sexy voice drawled in an unmistakeably American accent.

'Sorry.' She looked up into a pair of twinkling tawny eyes that laughed at her from a ruggedly handsome face, topped by thick, light brown hair with sun-kissed highlights. Phwoarr! was her immediate reaction, but she quickly pulled herself together. She'd just spilt coffee over this guy, for goodness sake, the least she could do was apologise instead of drooling over him like a lunatic.

'I'm so sorry,' she apologised again. 'I was looking at that yacht over there. It's fantastic, isn't it? I've never seen one like that before.' Not the thing to say, Amber, she scolded herself. You're supposed to be acting smart and sophisticated as if you come to these sort of events all the time, not twittering away like an idiot and letting the first person you bump into know that you've never seen anything bigger than a dinghy before. Then she remembered that she had quite literally 'bumped' into this man and drowned him in coffee in the process.

'Gosh, I'm so sorry,' she said, fully aware that this was the third time she'd apologised but unable to stop herself gabbling. She looked down at his wet denim cut-offs, trying not to let her gaze linger on the sun-tanned legs below them, then shifted her eyes hurriedly back to his face. 'Er, I'll go and get a cloth so you can clean up.'

'No need. I'm working on that yacht you were admiring so I haven't got far to go and get changed,' he replied. 'Perhaps you'd like to join me and clean yourself up too? You don't want to leave that to stain. It'll ruin your dress.'

What? She glanced down in confusion and saw that coffee was splattered all over the bottom of her – or rather, Callie's – dress and running down her legs. How could she have not noticed? *Because I was too busy gawping at him, that's why.*

She hesitated. He had said he was working on the yacht, which meant he didn't own it – more's the pity. So his boss could well be on board. And whilst the 'How to Hook a Millionaire' book Callie had brought and insisted she read from cover to cover had declared she should 'seize any opportunity to mix with the seriously rich' – and let's face it, anyone who owned that yacht was seriously rich – meeting them with a coffee-stained dress and legs was not a good idea. 'Always be perfectly made up and elegantly dressed' was another rule.

'Is your boss on board?' she asked.

'No, only me.' He was looking at her intently. 'Perhaps I should introduce myself, I'm sure your mother drilled it into you to never go off with strangers.' He held out his hand. 'Jed Curtess.'

She took his hand. It was strong and warm and his touch sent tingles running up her arm. 'Amber Wynters,' she told him.

'Now we've been introduced, Amber Wynters, would you like to come on board and get cleaned up?' he asked, a playful smile hovering on his lips.

She most definitely *would* but *should* she? She didn't even know this man, although she had to admit that she definitely found him appealing. Should she risk going onto the yacht with him? He might not be as harmless as he seemed. She saw the teasing twinkle in his gorgeous tawny eyes and her heart flipped. Cancel harmless. This guy was a danger to her blood pressure if nothing else.

'I promise I won't try to seduce you,' he said solemnly. 'Unless you beg me to, of course.' His eyes danced with humour and she thought there was probably a queue of women who would love him to do just that.

Something about this guy made her feel she could trust him. Besides, there were lots of people around to hear her shouts if she needed help – not that she would step one foot on that yacht if she felt in any danger. Anyway, she further convinced herself, she was supposed to be here to meet a millionaire and she wasn't about to do that in the state she was in.

'OK, thank you,' she agreed.

It was a fantastic yacht. Amber gazed around in undisguised, wide-eyed wonder as Jed led her onto the deck then down an elegant spiral suitcase to the foyer below. The interior was made of light-coloured, highly polished wood and her feet sank into the thick royal blue carpet that covered the floor. She slid off her strappy white sandals and wriggled her toes into the luxurious carpet.

'It's lovely and soft,' she said, smiling in delight. She picked up the sandals and dangled them on her fingertips. 'You're American, aren't you? Has your boss sailed this yacht all the way from America just for the Morgan Cup?'

According to Callie, the famous yacht race was held in Coombe Bay every year and people came from all over the world to take part or watch. It was one of the reasons they had taken up Callie's Aunt Sophie's offer to stay in her waterfront apartment while she visited her friends in Spain for a week. Callie had said it was the perfect opportunity for Amber to net a millionaire husband – and for Callie to have a lot of fun too, of course.

'No, he took a break from work for a while to sail around the world. His last stop was England. We sailed around the coast a bit then thought we'd stop by to see the race, but my boss had to fly back home to sort out something to do with his business, so he left me to take the yacht back.'

'You mean you're sailing it back to America all by yourself?' she asked.

'Sure. How come that surprises you so much? Don't I look like I can handle a yacht?' he drawled, obviously amused.

She hadn't meant to sound so rude. When would she

learn to think before she spoke? She shook her head. 'It isn't that. I was just surprised that a rich man like your boss travels with so little staff.'

Something flickered over Jed's face but was gone before she could figure out what it was. 'Sometimes he gets sick of being looked after and toadied to and wants to fend for himself,' he told her.

'Well, I don't blame him, I'm sure I'd feel the same,' she replied, hastily. 'Now, where's the bathroom? My legs are all sticky.'

'The guest bedroom is down that corridor, second door on your left,' he pointed. 'I'll use the bathroom in the master suite.'

She's beautiful, Jed thought as he watched Amber pad across the foyer, her sandals still dangling from her fingers. With her delicate elfin face, wide fudge-brown eyes, and wavy honey-brown hair that fell into waves just above her shoulders, she appeared every inch a society girl. But something about her didn't quite ring true. The dress she was wearing was obviously designer and her make-up was skilfully applied but he had a feeling that she wasn't as sophisticated as she appeared. It was the way she'd gazed around the yacht, her eyes wide with wonder at the splendour of it, frankly admitting that she'd never been on a yacht in her life, the way she talked and acted, so natural, so animated, so disarmingly honest. Usually the women who hung around the yachts and boat races were gold-diggers, hoping to hook themselves a millionaire. But although Amber certainly looked the part, her face was too honest, her manner too natural. She was like a breath of fresh air, and he was intrigued as to what she was doing here by herself.

'What a gorgeous bathroom,' she said when she returned, her legs and dress now coffee-free, although there was a large wet patch on her dress where the spilled drink had been. 'All that wonderful marble and glass.'

'Thank you. I'll pass your comments onto my boss, he chose the décor himself,' Jed told her.

'What's it like working for a millionaire?' she asked. Her tone was direct, as was her gaze. He sensed that the answer was important to her.

He shrugged casually. 'I do my job and get paid for it, same as everyone else.'

'Yes, but how does he treat you? You know what they say about millionaires, they've got so much money they don't think they have to try to be nice. They're supposed to be awful to work for, selfish, arrogant, demanding ...' Her voice trailed off, as if she suddenly thought that she shouldn't be talking like this.

'Really?' he raised an eyebrow enquiringly, trying to hide his amusement. She looked so awkward and a tell-tale blush was creeping up her neck. 'And how many millionaires do you know?'

'None at all,' she admitted and smiled sheepishly. 'Sorry. I shouldn't stereotype, should I?'

'I'm sure that lots of rich people are like that,' he told her. He knew they were, he'd met them. 'Now, would you like a cool drink before you go?'

'That would be lovely, thank you.'

As they sat on the deck, drinking chilled orange juice, Amber wondered what Callie would think if she could see her now. She hadn't seen Simon's yacht but she was sure it couldn't be any more luxurious than this one. Shame Jed isn't a millionaire, she thought wistfully. He seemed so nice.

Listen to me. I sound so mercenary. If anyone had told her two months ago that she would be looking for a millionaire to marry she'd have laughed in their face.

'So what are you doing wandering around by yourself?'

Jed's sexy drawl broke into her thoughts.

'I came with a friend but she's gone off for a sail with her boyfriend.' Her tone was casual. 'I'm meeting up with her later.'

'Do you like sailing? Or is it the millionaires that attract you?'

She felt the colour rush to her cheek. Was she that obvious?

'Sorry, that was rude of me,' he apologised.

'Yes, it was,' she said, struggling to regain her composure. 'My friend Callie and I are staying at her aunt's waterside apartment for a week because she's visiting friends in Spain, so we thought we'd take a look around while we're here. I've never been to this part of Devon before.' It was near enough the truth.

To her relief, someone chose that moment to ring her on her mobile. 'Sorry.' She took the phone out of her bag and looked at the name on the dial. It was Callie.

'It's my friend. I guess she's back from her sail and wants to me to meet her somewhere.' She swiped to answer the call.

'Hi, Callie ...'

She frowned as Callie explained that she and Simon had been invited to a party on one of the yachts and they wanted Amber to come too.

'I don't fancy it. I don't know anyone and I'll just be a gooseberry,' Amber said. She chewed her bottom lip as Callie tried to persuade her.

'You must come. This is your chance to meet someone. There's be lots of rich people there,' Callie insisted. 'We'll meet you by that café overlooking the marina in fifteen minutes.' She cut off before Amber could protest further.

'Is there anything wrong?' Jed asked. 'You look a bit worried.'

'Callie and Simon have been invited to a party and they want me to come too,' she told him.

'Don't you like parties?'

'Not really,' she admitted. 'Especially when I don't know anyone and they're all so ... rich.'

'Do you have a problem with rich people?'

She met his gaze. After all, what did she have to lose by telling him the truth? It wasn't as if he was a millionaire, so she didn't have to impress him.

'I've never mixed with any,' she admitted.

'But your friend has?'

'She's a model and her parents are quite well off, she's used to mixing with all sorts of people. She's a lot more sophisticated than I am.'

'Would you like me to come with you? Just for moral support. No strings attached.'

Now there was a thought. Jed was friendly and he was used to mixing with millionaires. She'd definitely feel more confident if he was besides her. And she wouldn't feel so desperate either if she turned up with a partner.

'I'd love you to, if you're sure you don't mind.' She glanced at his shorts and T-shirt. They weren't exactly party attire. 'I have to meet them in fifteen minutes.'

He caught her drift. 'It'll only take me ten minutes to shower and change,' he told her. 'And don't worry about me showing you up. I can wear some of my boss's clothes. We're the same size.'

Him show her up? He'd look sensational whatever he wore. 'OK, that'd be great,' she said, smiling at him.

She tried not to think of him in the shower. There was no doubt about it, although no other guy had even remotely appealed to her since she split with Rod, she was definitely attracted to Jed. Something about him got right under her skin. *Get a grip. Just because you've finally got over Rod there's no need to go ga-ga over the first handsome guy you meet.*

True to his word, Jed was back in ten minutes, freshly shaved and dressed in designer jeans, an off-white, short-sleeved shirt, and a pair of expensive brown leather casual shoes – Italian, no doubt.

'Will I do?' he asked, striking a model pose, which made her giggle.

Do? He was perfect. 'You certainly scrub up well,' she said.

'Thank you, mademoiselle.' He gave a mock bow. 'Now, I believe we have an important party to go to.'

As if on cue, her mobile rang. It was Callie again.

'We're just coming,' Amber told her.

'We?' Callie's voice sharpened.

'I'm bringing a friend,' Amber replied airily. 'See you in a few minutes.' She ended the call before Calista could question her further.

Callie and Simon were standing outside the same café where Amber had collided with Jed. Simon, tall, dark-haired, handsome in a classic kind of way, and at least ten years older than Callie, looked slightly bored. Callie, her hand shading her eyes from the sun, was scanning the crowd – obviously for her, Amber thought.

Amber raised her hand and was about to shout, but realised that wasn't really sophisticated so clamped her mouth shut. She glanced at Jed to see if he'd noticed her action but, to her relief he was busy staring at Callie. Callie had that effect on people.

'Is that Callie with the black hair and a light blue dress?' he asked.

'Yes. Gorgeous, isn't she?'

'Her boyfriend seems a bit attentive,' Jed observed as Simon possessively grabbed Callie's arm.

'There you are, Amber,' Callie flashed a devastating smile at Jed. 'And who's this?'

'Jed Curtess.' Jed held out his hand.

Amber felt a pang of jealousy as Callie shook Jed's hand, her eyes lingering on his for a moment. She fancies him, she thought. But then who wouldn't? He probably fancied her too.

Then it was Simon's turn to shake hands. 'Simon Purvell. Are you here for the race, Jed?' he asked.

'No, I'm looking after my boss's yacht.'

'And who's your boss? Perhaps I know him.'

'I doubt it. He lives in America,' Jed replied.

'Now, you two, no talking business. We're supposed to be going to a party, remember?' Callie said, pouting prettily as she clung to Simon's arm.

'Where exactly is this party?' asked Jed.

'On Guy's yacht – Lord Guy Turner – I expect you've heard of him?' Simon informed him. 'His son Randy is a good friend of mine.'

'Can't say I have.' Jed shook his head. 'Still, it's always a pleasure to meet someone new.'

He tucked Amber's arm inside his, sending shivers up her arm. 'Lead the way.'

I wish I wasn't so intensively aware of him, Amber thought as they walked along the marina. She was sure Jed could sense she was attracted to him and was enjoying it. She'd have to get herself under control before they arrived at this party.

A motor boat was waiting at the marine to take them out to Sir Guy's luxury yacht, which was moored out at sea. Amber had been impressed by Jed's boss's yacht but this one was stupendous, she thought as they went on board. It was huge, five stories high, and the inside was decorated in ivory, marble, and glass with expensive Persian carpets. A domed gold leaf ceiling was the high point of the guest lounge, where a huge, plasma screen TV dominated one wall and the inlaid wooden floor was scattered with Persian rugs. This was where the party was taking place. Amber stopped to look at an oil painting on one wall.

'That's an original, isn't it?' she asked. '*The Hay Wain*

has always been my favourite Constable.'

'Mine too,' a voice said behind her.

Turning, she saw a middle-aged, aristocratic-looking man, still quite handsome with a full head of silver hair. 'Lord Guy Taylor,' he said, holding out his hand. 'Glad to meet you all. Any friends of Simon's and all that.' His smile encompassed the whole group. 'Make yourselves at home and help yourselves to drinks.'

'Would you like a glass of champagne, madam?'

A waiter was standing beside her, holding a silver tray full of glasses of the sparkling drink.

I bet this champagne is the expensive stuff, not like the cheap bottles I get from the supermarket, she thought, taking a glass. 'Thank you'. She sipped it cautiously; it tasted good, bubbly, and refreshing.

The waiter handed Jed, Callie, and Simon a glass of champagne too, then moved onto the next group of guests.

'Look, there's Sadie and Karl! We must go and talk to them. See you later, you two,' Callie said.

She dragged Simon off, leaving Amber with Jed, who was deep in a conversation about sailing with Sir Guy. Amber hovered politely, feeling a bit awkward. Jed caught her eye and smiled apologetically. She smiled back to reassure him and took a sip of the champagne for Dutch courage. She had never been anywhere like this before. The place shouted money and so did the guests. All the women were beautiful and sophisticated, dressed in designer clothes and expensive jewellery, laughing and chatting, perfectly at ease. All except her. She was wearing her friend's clothes and was here under false pretences. She was here to bag a millionaire. Callie belonged with these people, her family were aristocrats, she had been brought up with money. Whereas Amber was a fraud, an impostor, a gold-digger. What's more, she was sure that everyone in the room realised it.

Panic seized her. She had to get out of here. She turned

to tell Jed that she'd like to go home but a beautiful blonde in a red dress that left little to the imagination was now talking animatedly to him.

'I don't think we've met before.'

She looked up at the tall, fair-haired man in front of her. He was about her age and handsome, in a film star sort of way, his sun-kissed hair falling loosely over his face so his piercing blue eyes were barely visible. He pushed his hair back with his hand and gave her the full benefit of his charming smile, obviously aware of how good it made him look.

'In fact, I know we haven't met. There's no way I'd forget you.' His eyes raked her body then rested on her face. 'I'm Randy Turner.' He gave her a disarming smile, holding her in his gaze.

Turner. Of course, she could see the resemblance. 'So this is your father's yacht?' she asked. Her cheeks felt hot and she hoped she wasn't blushing.

'Yes, and one day it will be mine.' He took a long, slow sip from the glass of champagne he was holding, his eyes never leaving her face. 'And how about you, will you be mine?'

'Pardon?' She stared at him. *For goodness sake, pull yourself together, Amber, it's only a chat up line. You're supposed to be acting cool and sophisticated.* She took a big gulp of her drink to give herself courage, then realised that she'd emptied the glass.

Randy half-turned, clicked his fingers, and a waiter walked over. The waiter took a glass of champagne off the silver tray he was holding and handed it to Amber, taking her empty glass from her.

'Thank you.' She held the stem of the glass tightly in her hand.

'Well?' Randy raised an eyebrow arrogantly. 'You haven't answered my question. 'You're not going out with anyone are you? That guy you arrived with?'

'Jed? No, he's just ... an acquaintance.' Amber took another sip of champagne and tried to act sophisticated. Honestly, anyone would think she'd never been chatted up before.

'Good, then there's nothing stopping you going out with me, is there?'

This was going way too fast for her. She'd only been on the yacht ten minutes and already she had a millionaire's son asking her for a date. She remembered what the book had said, play it cool.

'I'll have to consult my diary,' she said flippantly.

'I'd better warn you that I'm used to getting what I want.' He smiled disarmingly.

'Funny, so am I.' She finished her champagne and held out the empty glass. 'And right now, I'd like another drink.' *Steady, Amber, that will be your third. Better sip it slowly.*

Randy clicked his fingers again and the waiter hurried over to replace both their empty glasses.

'Drink up, then I'll give you a tour of the yacht,' he said.

Something told her that wouldn't be a good idea. She didn't trust him, he was too smooth an operator. Besides, she was feeling a bit light-headed. Too much champagne on top of an empty stomach, she guessed, realising that she'd had nothing to eat all day.

'Actually ...' she tried to think of an excuse.

'There you are, darling.' Jed appeared by her side and planted a kiss on her cheek that made her senses reel. He gently but firmly took hold of her arm. 'Sorry to interrupt but there's someone I'd like you to meet.' He nodded at Randy then whisked Amber away.

'What do you think you're doing?' she demanded, her cheek still burning from that kiss.

'I thought you needed rescuing. Randy looks a right slime-ball. I can guess what kind of guided tour he had in mind,' Jed said.

'So can I. Which is why I was about to refuse to go with him. I don't need a bodyguard, you know.'

'Look, you don't realise what these people can be like. Some of them think money can buy anything and anyone. You're out of your depths with people like Randy Taylor.'

'Then I'm going to have to learn how to cope with them, aren't I?' she snapped. 'And how to tell the nice millionaires from the creepy ones. Like Callie does.'

'Your friend, if you'll forgive me saying so, seems a lot more worldly-wise than you do.' He glanced over at Callie, who was ardently kissing Simon in the corner of the room. 'Look, let's leave this party and go somewhere else for a meal, I bet you haven't eaten yet and you've been knocking back that champagne as if it's sparkling water.'

'No, I've to stay here,' she said trying to ignore the fact that her head was spinning dizzily. 'I have to meet a millionaire.'

'Why?' His voice was curt. 'Why exactly do you want to meet a millionaire, Amber?'

'Because I have to get one to marry me, and as quickly as possible.'

She saw his eyes widen with shock then her head spun dizzily and everything went black.

Chapter Two

Rule number 2: Act confident and sophisticated

Amber stirred. Her head was pounding and her throat was so dry it felt like sandpaper. For a moment she wondered what was wrong with her, then she remembered the party on Lord Guy's yacht, and realised with a groan that she'd got drunk and now had a massive hangover. She tried to cast her mind back to the party to recall if she'd done anything so embarrassing that she couldn't show her face in public again but everything was a blur. She couldn't even remember how she got home.

What she needed now was the loo, a glass of water – it would have been better if she'd drunk that before she went to bed then she might not have this hangover – and a cup of coffee, in that order. Actually, the loo was top priority. She opened her eyes, pushed back the duvet in order to get out of bed, then gasped. This wasn't her room! And, what was even worse, she was dressed in her undies!

In a panic she looked around for her dress and saw it folded neatly over the back of a chair. Her white handbag was placed on the seat of the chair and her strappy sandals side by side underneath the chair. Who had put them there? Where was she? Oh, if only her head would stop thudding and she could remember what had happened.

Forcing herself to keep calm, she looked around to see if anything jogged her memory. She was sitting on the end of a massive king-size bed, covered by a cream linen duvet. She turned to see if the other side of the bed had been slept in and was relieved to see there was no indent in the large pumped-up pillow. She scanned the room, staring at the curtains, the thick gold carpet, the expensive light wood – maple, was it? – wardrobe and cupboards. None of it was familiar.

Where was she?

And where was the loo? Rising slowly to her feet, she clutched her stomach as it lurched in protest, wishing she didn't feel so dizzy. Then she realised the room was swaying. Surely she wasn't still on the luxury yacht with, she frowned as she tried to recall his name – Randy, that was it. She remembered vaguely that he'd offered to give her a guided tour. Had she been so drunk she'd taken him up on his offer? What had happened then? Oh, if only she hadn't drunk so much of that perishing champagne. Surely she hadn't ...

A knock on the door made her jump. She scrambled back into bed and sat up with the duvet pulled over her shoulders. It seemed that she was about to find out exactly whose yacht she was on.

'Come in!' she croaked, her eyes fixed on the door.

Heart pounding she watched as the handle turned and the door slowly opened. Then, to her amazement and relief, Jed came in, carrying a tray on which she could see a glass of water, a glass of orange juice, and a plate of buttered toast.

'How's your head?' he asked as he walked over to the bed.

'Throbbing.' Amber clutched the duvet closer. 'Er, I can't seem to remember much of last night,' she confessed.

He sat down on the end of the bed. 'I'm not surprised, the amount of champagne you were knocking back,' he said unsympathetically.

'I was nervous,' she told him. 'And I'm not used to drinking champagne. I didn't realise how lethal it is. And I hadn't eaten,' she added.

'I suspected as much.' He took a small container off the tray and shook out two tables. 'Here, these painkillers will make you feel better.' He handed her the tablets and a glass of water.

How was she going to take them off him and keep hold of the duvet at the same time?

Securing the duvet in place with one hand, she reached out for the tablets, popped them in her mouth, then took the glass. 'Thanks,' she said when she'd finally managed to swallow them. Trouble is, now her need to go to the loo was even more urgent.

'No problem. I'll leave you to eat your breakfast.' He put the tray down on the bedside cabinet, then pointed to a door on the left. 'The en suite's through there if you want the bathroom and a shower, and you'll find some clothes in the wardrobe that'll probably fit you if you want to change into anything fresh. They belong to my boss's wife.'

'Thanks,' she mumbled again, her cheeks growing hot. She was dying to ask him what happened last night but she needed the loo so desperately she didn't dare keep him talking. Besides, she'd rather face those sort of questions when she was fully dressed and feeling a bit stronger.

'I'll be on the deck if you need me,' he told her as he went out.

Fifteen minutes later, showered and dressed in a gorgeous lemon designer dress that she'd found in the wardrobe, Amber tried to recollect her thoughts. Randy had been plying her with champagne, she could remember that. And she had a vague memory of talking to Jed a little later but after that her mind went blank. She just hoped she hadn't acted stupid at the party and shown herself up. She couldn't even remember how she'd got on Jed's yacht, never mind undressed and in his spare bed. At least, she hoped it was his spare bed.

She opened her bag, took out her lipstick, and applied a thin smear to her lips. Shame she hadn't got the rest of her make up with her, she could do with some armour right now. Thankfully she had her sunglasses. They would serve both to shield her eyes against the glare of the light and to mask her embarrassment. She donned them then went in search of Jed.

As she'd guessed, he was up on deck, lying on a sun lounger, reading the newspaper. He glanced up as she approached. 'Feeling better?'

'Yes, thanks, though my head is still killing me,' She sat down on a deck chair by the table. 'I hope I didn't make too much of a fool of myself last night,' she said awkwardly.

He folded the paper and put it on the table. 'You passed out before you could do anything really stupid,' he reassured her. 'I looked for your friend but couldn't find her. I didn't know the address of the cottage you were staying at so thought it best to bring you back here.'

'I see.' She swallowed. *Keep calm, Amber, just ask him.* 'Look, this is going to sound awful but I have to know. I can't remember much about last night, you see, and I wondered ... er ...' She felt her cheeks burn. Damn, she was making a mess of this. Callie would have handled it with much more sophistication.

'You want to know if we spent the night together?' He sounded amused.

'Well, yes.'

'No, we didn't. I'm not in the habit of taking advantage of women who are too drunk to know what they're doing, no matter how beautiful they are.

'Good, because I'm not that kind of girl,' she said firmly.

'Not unless I happen to be a millionaire,' he replied.

'What?' She shot him a worried glance, grateful her sunglasses hid her eyes.

He reached out and took the sunglasses off her face. 'You told me last night that you had to marry a millionaire.' His tawny eyes stared intently into hers. 'But you passed out before you could tell me why.'

'Oh no,' she groaned, biting her lip. 'I didn't, did I? Did anyone else hear me?'

'No, your secret's safe with me. But you seemed to think that it was a matter of urgency and you don't strike me as the stereotypical gold-digger. So what exactly is the reason you feel obliged to take such drastic action?'

She flinched at the word 'gold-digger' but he was right, that's what she was. She hated Jed to think of her in that way, to believe that she was just looking for a meal ticket like some of the other girls she saw hanging around the yachts. For some reason she cared what he thought about her. So she found herself telling him how she'd discovered that her parents were struggling financially because her father – a self-employed plumber who had been fit and hearty all his life so hadn't seen the need for health insurance – had a very sudden and unexpected heart attack that left him too ill to work. And how, thanks to Rod, the creepy, two-timing rat she had been engaged to, they were about to lose their home. A beautiful Tudor house that had been in the family for generations. 'Unknown to me, Rod persuaded Dad to put his savings into shares, but they went bust,' she explained. 'My dad adores that house. It will break his heart to sell. And it's all my fault. Dad only trusted Rod because he was engaged to me.'

'Do your parents blame you?' Jed asked softly.

She shook her head. 'I don't think so. They keep telling me not to blame myself but how can I ignore the fact that it's my ex fiancé that got them in this mess? So it's up to me to do all I can to pay them back and marrying a millionaire is the only way I can do it.' She raised her eyes to his. 'I know it sounds so mercenary but I'm scared the stress of having to sell the house will cause my dad to

19

have another heart attack. I'll never forgive myself if anything happens to him.'

She's either a very good actress or deadly serious. Jed leant back and surveyed her thoughtfully.

'What about love?' he asked.

'Pardon?' She asked, startled.

'Well, people usually marry for love. I gather you're intending to marry someone you don't love?'

'It might be a better bet than marrying someone I do love,' she snapped back at him. 'I almost did that with Rod and look where it got me. He went off with someone else and bankrupted my parents into the bargain.' She shook her head. 'No, I'm not letting my heart rule my head again. Callie was right, marrying a millionaire is the only option I've got.'

'So this was your friend's idea, was it?'

'Callie's been so helpful. She let me borrow her clothes and she said all I have to do is look the part and follow the guide in the book.'

'What book?'

Flushing a little, she explained about a book called 'How to Hook a Millionaire' which she and Callie had been studying the past couple of weeks.

He could hardly believe it. 'You mean someone's actually written a book to tell women how to ensnare a millionaire and you and your friend are following its advice?' he asked incredulously.

'Well ... yes.' Her cheeks were practically glowing.

'So you're going to do everything this book says? Deceive someone? Pretend you love him so you can get hold of their money?' He could barely keep the contempt out of his voice.

'No, I won't, I'd never do that!' Anger flashed in her eyes. 'I wouldn't tell anyone I loved them if I didn't. I know how it feels.'

He saw the look of pain on her face and reached out to put his hand over hers, fighting back the urge to take her in his arms and kiss her. Something he'd wanted to do all the day before. Especially last night when, without warning, she'd slipped off her dress and climbed into bed, seeming to completely forget he was standing beside her. It had taken all his willpower to turn around and walk out of the room. 'I guess this Rod really hurt you, eh?'

She nodded, her eyes now clouding over. 'I was stupid. If I hadn't been so infatuated I'd have seen what he was like.'

'We've all been guilty of that at some time in our life,' he told her. *I certainly have*, he thought, remembering Melissa. Luckily, he'd found out before he proposed that she was just after him for his money. That had hurt for a long, long time. He detested the women who hung about the haunts of the rich and successful, hoping to ensnare themselves a wealthy husband. Just like Amber was planning to do. 'But can't you see, noble as your reasons are, you can't marry someone just because they've got loads of money. It's not fair.'

She pulled her hands away from his and stood up, her chin tilted defiantly. 'I'll do whatever I have to do to help my parents. I owe them that. And if I do manage to get a millionaire to propose to me – which is highly unlikely with the amount of competition about and the limited amount of time I have – I'll be perfectly fair. I won't cheat on him. I'll be a loyal and supportive wife.' Her voice was laced with anger. 'Now, if you don't mind, I think it's time I went home. I'll have this dress cleaned and return it to you by the end of the week.

'There's no need. Keep it if you like,' he offered.

'No thank you. I wouldn't want you to think I'd deliberately stayed the night on your yacht so I could get a free designer dress,' she retorted.

Picking up her bag, she flounced off.

Let her go, he thought. Women like her weren't worth chasing.

How dare he sit and judge me? Amber thought as she walked back to Callie's aunt's house. *He's right*, a niggling little voice said inside her head. *You are being a gold-digger.* But what else could she do? Stand by and watch her parents lose their home because of her? She thought of the beautiful Tudor building where she'd grown up, as had her father, grandfather, and great grandfather. Was what she was doing so bad? After all, the rich often married for profitable reasons, didn't they? To merge their companies and other business reasons. Why shouldn't she marry for convenience too?

'Amber, thank goodness you're home,' Callie said as soon as Amber walked through the door. 'I've been so worried about you. I tried to phone you but kept getting a message saying your number was unavailable.'

'Really?' Amber took her mobile out of her bag and saw that the screen was blank. Her battery had run down. 'Oh, my mobile needs charging, that's why you couldn't get me.'

'I was looking for you last night. Randy said that you'd got a bit drunk so Jed had taken you home,' Callie continued. 'I got in late so went straight to bed. When I got up this morning and found that you hadn't been back I was worried sick.'

'I'm afraid I was too drunk to tell Jed where I lived,' Amber confessed. 'So I spent the night on his yacht – in separate rooms,' she added hastily, seeing the look on her friend's face.

'So Jed's boss keeps a supply of clothes on his yacht in case anyone stays overnight?' Callie asked. She'd obviously noticed the dress Amber was wearing.

'There's a wardrobe full of stuff, toiletries, make up, the lot,' Amber told her. 'They belong to Jed's boss's wife.'

'I hope you're not getting too keen on this Jed. Remember he only works for a millionaire, he isn't one. Whereas Randy is seriously rich and he's quite taken with you,' Callie added.

'How do you know?' Amber asked.

'He wouldn't stop talking about you last night. And Simon told me that Randy's father is anxious for him to marry and settle down. So this could be your big chance.'

Amber thought about marrying Randy. She hadn't been too impressed last night. He was handsome enough, sexy too, more in a superfluous way than a sense-reeling way like Jed.

When had she noticed that about Jed?

Then she realised that Callie was still talking. 'So they'll be here in an hour,' she said.

'What? Who'll be here?'

'Simon and Randy. They're taking us out for lunch.' Callie scrutinised her. 'That dress is perfect, but you need to put some make-up on. And don't get drunk again. You're supposed to be confident and sophisticated.'

'I don't usually get drunk, as you know,' Amber said defensively. 'I was just so nervous and I didn't realise how potent the champagne was. *And* I'd eaten nothing all day.' She sat down. 'I don't think I can pull this off, Callie. I'm not confident and sophisticated and I never will be. So why on earth would a man like Randy, who's loaded and can have any woman he wants, want to marry me?'

'Because you are going to make him want you,' said Callie. 'Remember the ten rules. All you have to do is keep to them and he'll be putty in your hands.'

Amber watched as Callie expertly applied baby pink nail varnish to her perfectly buffed false nails. Her friend might be at home in this sophisticated world of fast living, designer clothes, expensive yachts, 'Hooray Henry's', and champagne cocktails but she wasn't. She was a hot chocolate and slippers by the fire kind of girl. She didn't see how she was going to fool anyone otherwise.

Callie was right, Randy is definitely interested in me, Amber thought as she returned home much later that afternoon. That was clear from the way he'd been all over her at lunch at the yacht club, not wanting to leave her side and practically insisting she join him at the private party held at the yacht that evening. Callie and Simon were going to so Amber had agreed. However, she had to admit that, although Randy was pleasant enough, she wasn't attracted to him.

Not like she was to Jed.

Well, she had to forget about Jed. She had to marry someone seriously rich, not a hired hand.

'Apparently, Randy turns thirty next year, and he comes into a huge sum of money – hundreds of thousands – if he's married with a baby by then. And his father has promised to give him another fifty thousand as a wedding present,' Callie told her. 'You need to make a big effort tonight, Amber. You've got to make sure you're the prettiest, sexiest, wittiest, and most fun girl at the party.'

'Is that all?' Amber stifled a yawn. 'I've got no chance of doing that. Maybe I should just give it a miss.'

'Do you want to save your precious family home from being sold? Because Randy is your only chance of doing that.'

Callie always did say things how they were. 'I was only joking. Of course I'm going to the party. And I'll do everything in my power to convince Randy that I'm the woman for him. OK?'

'Good. Remember what the book says. "Once you've got him interested don't let him go". In fact, I think we'd better go over the main points in the book. This could be an important night for you.'

Amber groaned. The last thing she wanted to do was

read through that tiresome book again, but she knew better than argue with Callie. 'OK, but at least let me have a cup of coffee first. Want one?'

'A skinny latté please. I'll highlight some things for you to remember while you make it,' Callie replied, reaching to pick up the 'Millionaire Book' from under the coffee table.

Amber sighed and went into the kitchen to put the kettle on. Then she glanced at her mobile phone and saw a missed call from her mother – two hours ago. Worried that something had happened to her father, she dialled the number.

'Oh, Amber, thank you for getting back to me dear.' Her mother's voice sounded wobbly. 'Your father said not to bother you but I thought you ought to know. After all, it's your childhood home, you still have things here …'

'What is it?' Amber asked anxiously.

'Well, the bank has foreclosed, dear. We have to sell the house. We had some estate agents around and it's going on the market tomorrow. '

'Oh, Mum. I'm so sorry. Is there nothing we can do?'

'I'm afraid not, dear, but I don't want you to worry. We'll be fine. There'll be some money left over to buy us a little place. I just wanted to let you know. That's all. I'll not keep you talking. I'm sure you've got lots to do. Have a lovely time.' And she was gone.

Amber knew that although her mother was trying to put on a brave face, she was dreadfully upset. That's why she'd got off the phone so quickly. And her father would be devastated.

I can't let this happen, she vowed. Callie was right, she had to make a play for Randy, especially as he was so obviously interested in her. And by the sound of it, they'd both be doing each other a favour. She made the coffee and carried it into the lounge.

'Right. What does the book say I do next?' she asked.

He knew she'd be there. He'd heard Randy and Simon talking at the bar in the yacht club lunchtime, discussing how they were taking the 'fillies', as they called Callie and Amber, to the dance that was being held there later that evening. Jed hadn't planned on going to the dance himself. It wasn't his scene. But the image of Amber dancing in Randy's arms kept flashing across his mind and in the end he donned a dinner jacket and set off.

He spotted Amber as soon as he walked in, standing by the bar, talking to Randy. She looked breathtakingly beautiful in a slinky black strapless dress that hugged her body like a glove. As she walked over to a nearby table where Callie and Simon were sitting, he noticed the dress had a slit up one side that gave a tantalising glimpse of her shapely thigh. Watching her, his stomach tightened and his body instantly responded to the sensuous sway of her hips. *Cool it. That girl is only interested in marrying someone with money,* he reminded himself firmly.

As if she could sense him, Amber suddenly stopped, half-turned, and glanced over. Their eyes met and locked. For a moment everything and everyone else seemed obliterated, as if they were the only two in the room. Then she smiled, waved, and turned away to continue walking over to the table.

It took him a moment or two to pull himself together. *Get a grip, Curtess.*

Someone clapped him on the shoulder. 'Jed, my lad, glad you could make it!'

It was Lord Guy. He and Jed had got talking the other night at the party on board his yacht, and Jed had found him entertaining company.

'Lord Guy,' Jed nodded. 'Good to see you again.'

'Come and join me for a drink,' Lord Guy invited him. 'There's a couple of people I'd like you to meet. They'll be interested in your travels, they do a lot of sailing themselves.'

Amber forced herself not to turn around and stare at him. He'd looked so handsome in that dinner suit that it had taken all her willpower to tear her eyes off him. The way he'd looked at her had unnerved her, like he could see right through her, read her mind. Not that he could, of course. Which was good because she didn't want him finding out just how much she was attracted to him.

All evening, as she was chatting to Randy, Callie, and Simon, Amber was so aware of Jed. It was like all her senses were on alert, listening and watching for him. She longed for him to join them, yet dreaded it too because she knew that he disapproved of what she was planning to do. As far as he was concerned, she was just a gold-digger. *Well, damn him*, she thought, angrily. Who was he to judge her? All she was trying to do was look after her parents. After all, she was responsible for getting them in this mess and her dad's health was so fragile.

'Shall we join them?' Randy asked her as Callie and Simon headed for the dance floor.

Amber hesitated. She wasn't very good at dancing. Not proper close up dancing like this. The only dancing she'd done was jiggling about to the latest hit at a disco when she was in her teens. Still, it couldn't be that difficult. Everyone else was managing fine.

'Sure.' She nodded, getting up and taking his outstretched hand.

It was a slow number so Randy took her in his arms and led the way around the dance floor. He smelt of expensive aftershave and alcohol and held her close. Too close. She felt awkward and constantly stepped on his feet or danced out of tune. *Oh, great work, Amber*, she scolded herself as she slipped up once again. *You're supposed to be acting cool and sophisticated and you can't even keep in step to a simple tune.*

'You haven't done much dancing, have you?' Randy sounded amused.

'Er, no ... it's not really my thing,' she replied.

'Maybe you should get a bit more practice,' he suggested.

'Maybe she just needs a better partner,' a familiar drawl cut in. 'Allow me.'

'Be my guest.' Randy released her. Then she was in Jed's arms and her senses were reeling at the sheer potent male scent of him, the closeness of his body, the feel of his skin against hers.

'Just relax and let me lead.' Jed pulled her close.

She let herself sink into his strong, powerful arms, moulded her body against his, followed his steps. To her delight, she actually managed to dance in step. She noticed Jed looking at her, his eyes twinkling with amusement, and realised that she was grinning like a loony just because she'd actually managed to get a few steps right. He must think she was so totally crass.

'See, it isn't that difficult, is it?' he asked as they swept across the dance floor.

'Not for you maybe.' She smiled up at him. 'I constantly seem to be doing things wrong. Do you know I actually went to drink out of the fingerbowl at dinner last night?' she confessed. 'I was just about to put it to my mouth when I saw Callie glaring at me and shaking her head.'

He chuckled, a deep, throaty chuckle as if he was really amused. 'Oh, Amber, why don't you just forget all this marrying a millionaire scheme and be yourself? You're too good to mix with half this crowd anyway. Most of them are just spoilt, self-indulgent, pompous snobs.'

'You know why,' she reminded him. 'And the situation is getting even more urgent. My mum phoned me today. They've had to put their house on the market. And a place like theirs will soon be snapped up. I've got to pay them back the money they've lost.'

The dance came to an end but Jed showed no sign of releasing her, evidently deciding she needed a bit more practise. The music started up again, another slow, smoochy number, and he led Amber around the dance floor. *He must have worked with his millionaire boss for some time,* Amber thought. He was so sure of himself, so at ease with these people, always knowing what to say and do. Though he had so much self-confidence that she doubted if he would care if he did or said anything that was wrong according to their rules anyway. He'd already made it obvious that what he thought about the 'rich set'.

In fact, Jed was just the person she needed to teach her how to act, she suddenly realised. Callie had given her some pointers, but she was far too busy enjoying herself with Simon to accompany Amber everywhere. Dare she suggest it to him? She could offer to pay him, not that she had money to spare but it would be an investment if it helped her hook Randy. And Jed must need the money if he had to wear his boss's clothes all the while.

'Ouch!' Jed winced as she stepped on his toe.

'Sorry,' she apologised, hastily. 'I was too busy thinking.' She hesitated.

'Oho, this looks serious,' he said. 'Shall we sit down?'

The music ended, and although Jed had released her, his hand was still resting on her arm as he guided her over to an empty table. She looked for Randy and saw him chatting to a tall, exotic-looking brunette at the bar.

'It won't hurt him to see you talking to another man,' Jed told her as they both sat down at the table. 'You don't want him taking you for granted, do you?'

'No, but I haven't got long to snare him,' Amber said. 'I'm only down here on holiday, remember?' She took a deep breath and looked Jed straight in the eye. 'So I was hoping you could help me.'

'Me?' he raised an eyebrow quizzically. 'Well, I've

never seen matchmaking as one of my many talents.'

'No, but you know how to act. You're so comfortable and relaxed with everyone,' she told him. 'You know how to talk to them and what to talk about, what knife and fork to use, how to dance, how to sail. You're just as home wearing a dinner suit in this posh yacht club as you are dressed in cut-off denims mucking about on your boss's boat. No one would guess you were just the hired hand.'

'Thanks, I think,' he said, a sarcastic edge to his voice. 'Where's this leading or are you just going to keep paying me compliments?'

'Well,' she swallowed. She didn't want him to laugh at her. 'I was wondering if you would be my adviser? Show me how to act and what to say so I fit in? I'd pay you, of course,' she added.

He looked at her thoughtfully for a minute, and her heart missed a beat. Would he turn her down?

'Is it really that important to you?' he asked. He glanced over at Randy, who was now weaving his way through the crowd, a glass of champagne in each hand. 'To marry someone like that creep?'

'Yes,' she said simply.

'OK, then I'll do it,' he told her. 'But I don't want your money. Call it a friendly favour.'

'Oh, but I couldn't …'

His eyes met hers, deadly serious. 'I either do it as a favour or not at all,' he told her.

'Then thank you, I accept.' she agreed.

'Right, well what's the next step in your "Millionaire Plan"?' he asked, briskly.

She thought quickly. She'd already done 'be seen at the right places' and 'act confident and sexy'' Well, tried to, anyway. What was rule three? She pulled the piece of paper that she'd written them all on out of her handbag. 'Take an interest in his work and hobbies so you can join in with them,' she read out.

'OK. Randy doesn't work and his hobbies are drinking, spending money, women, and sailing,' Jed told her. 'So we'll deal with the sailing as I'm sure you don't need my help with the others. Can you sail?'

She shook her head. 'I've never been sailing,' she confessed.

'Then I'll give you your first lesson tomorrow. Be at my yacht at ten o'clock.' He nodded and rose just as Randy approached the table. 'She's all yours. And she only stepped on my foot once.'

He walked away without waiting for a reply.

'I don't know what you see in that Jed, he's just a waster,' Randy grumbled as Amber rose from her seat. 'Are you coming back over to our table or not?'

'Yes, of course. Jed was just telling me about his travels. He and his boss have sailed across the world in that yacht, you know.'

'I've done a lot of sailing too,' Randy told her. 'In fact, a few of us are going sailing on Tuesday. Why don't you come along?'

The day after tomorrow? *What brilliant timing*, Amber thought. After her lesson with Jed tomorrow she'd be able to go sailing with Randy and not act like a complete novice.

'I'd love too, thanks,' she said.

'Nice one, trying to make Randy jealous by spending time with Jed,' Callie said when they were both touching up their make up in the ladies room. 'He's gorgeous, even if he isn't a millionaire. Randy was on edge all the time you were dancing.'

'I wasn't trying to make Randy jealous, Jed's just a friend,' Amber told her. 'He showed me how to dance and he's going to teach me how to sail tomorrow.'

Callie frowned. 'You shouldn't be spending too much time with him. Keeping Randy on his toes is one thing, but you don't want him to think you aren't interested, do you? You should be going sailing with Randy, not Jed.'

'I am, I'm going with him on Tuesday. That's why I'm going with Jed tomorrow, so he can teach me the ropes and make sure I don't make a complete fool of myself.'

'Well, just watch what you're doing. I've seen the way you look at Jed and how he looks at you. There's definitely something between you. Anyone can see that,' Callie replied.

'Don't be ridiculous, Jed and I are just friends. I'm not interested in him in that way at all.'

Liar.

OK, she was. But Jed wasn't interested in her and even if by some remote chance he was, there was no way she was going to blow her chance to marry Randy for a torrid affair with a nobody like Jed, no matter how sexy he is. No way at all.

Chapter Three

Rule number 3: Take an interest in his work and hobbies.

Great, she'd forgotten to check the name of Jed's – or rather his boss's – boat, Amber realised as she walked past rows of yachts moored along the marina front the next morning. Would she recognise it? It had stood out from the others, she remembered. It was noticing the yacht and looking for the name of it that made her tip the coffee over him in the first place!

To her relief she spotted it, and there painted across the side was the name *Chenoa*. She'd never come across that before - it must be foreign. *Probably a woman's name,* she thought. *His wife or girlfriend, perhaps*. It certainly gave the yacht an exotic feel to it.

She climbed up the steps and onto the deck. 'Hello? Anyone on board?'

There was no sign of Jed. He *had* told her to be here for ten o'clock, hadn't he? She slid the patchwork leather bag, containing a packed lunch, drinks, and essentials such as make-up and hairbrush, off her shoulder and looked around. Where was he?

Then she heard footsteps behind her and turned. Her stomach tightened as she saw him walking towards her dressed in just a pair of black Bermuda shorts, a smattering of curly dark hair covering his bare, sun-tanned chest. He was soo sexy!

She tore her gaze away from him. What was she doing, thinking about Jed like this? It was Randy she had to snare. Jed was just a friend.

'Good morning. Are you always this punctual?' he asked, smiling. 'I thought women were usually late.'

'I didn't want to keep you waiting, seeing as you've been kind enough to help me,' she replied, her voice sounding far more husky than she wanted it to. 'Any chance of a cold drink before we go?' she asked. She needed something to cool her down. In fact, she'd have to keep a bucket of ice nearby if Jed intended to spend the entire day clad only in those shorts. She was only human, after all, and anyone's temperature would rise faced with a body like that, even if they didn't fancy the guy. Which she didn't. Absolutely not.

'Of course, mineral water or orange juice?' he asked.

'Mineral water, please. With ice.'

By the time Jed came back with a sparkling glass of iced water, Amber had managed to regain her composure by telling herself that there was no need to make a big deal about the fact that she found him attractive, it was a perfectly natural reaction to a good-looking guy. So when she reached for the glass and their fingers touched she managed to ignore the electrifying tingle that ran up her arm and smile sweetly.

'Thank you.' She sipped the water, savouring its coldness. 'Where are we going today?'

'Blyte Nature Reserve. It's a little island just off the coast. Have you heard of it?' he asked.

She shook her head. 'What's there?'

'Mainly sea birds. They roost there every summer to breed. I'm going there because I need some photos of rare birds for an article I'm writing.'

'You write articles?' *There's no need to sound quite so surprised*, she chided herself.

He shrugged. 'Well, photography, especially wildlife, is my main interest but sometimes I'm asked to write an article to accompany the photos I take.'

'What magazine is this article for?' she asked. Jed

intrigued her. She had a feeling there was much more to him than he chose to let people know.

He named a popular wildlife magazine and she whistled. 'Impressive.'

'What about you?' he asked, leaning back against the rail, his arms folded across his chest. 'What do you do for a living?'

'I'm a graphic designer. I work for a small magazine that specialises in home designs.'

'Did you study at Art College?' he asked.

'I did a degree at Uni. I freelanced for a while but got sick of never knowing when I was getting paid so I took this job. At least I get a regular salary.' She shrugged. 'Anyway, enough about me. How far away is this Nature Reserve?'

'Only an hour or so. I thought that would be long enough to find out if you were going to be sea sick or not,' he said. 'I presume you'd want to know that before you sail off with Randy tomorrow.'

Sea sick – she hadn't thought of that! And he was right, she needed to know. It wouldn't look good if she was puking the entire time she went sailing with Randy. Definitely not the way to impress someone.

'I don't suffer from travel sickness in a car, so surely I'll be OK.'

'Maybe. You'd amazed how many people can travel OK by car or plane but as soon as the waves start rolling they feel ill,' he replied. 'Don't worry, I've got some good remedies on board in case you need them.'

She grimaced. 'Let's hope I don't.'

Jed smiled as he watched Amber struggle to fasten her life jacket – upside down and back to front. He knew he should point out her mistake right away instead of leaving her to struggle but she looked so cute, frowning with her tongue sticking out between her teeth, he couldn't take her eyes off her. She was so natural and uninhibited with him, obviously deciding that seeing as he wasn't a millionaire she didn't need to try and impress him. She was far too trusting and open for a spoilt, selfish moron like Randy. She deserved someone who would care for her, cherish her, love her, not use her to gain his inheritance. *She was using Randy too*, he reminded himself.

'There, done it!' she said. Her face glowing with triumph.

He tried to keep his face straight but failed miserably.

'What are you grinning at? Have I done it wrong?'

'Let's just say it's a good job we had this practise run today.'

He walked over to her and started to unfasten the jacket, but the proximity of her body unnerved him so much he fumbled. He was so totally aware of her, the exotic perfume she was wearing, the softness of her skin, the way her honey-brown hair tumbled onto her shoulders. *Get a grip, Curtess*, he told himself sharply and quickly unfastened the jacket.

'You've got it on upside down and back to front,' he explained. 'How about trying it again?' He didn't trust himself to take it off and put it on properly for her. Right now, it was all he could do to stop himself taking her in his arms and kissing her so passionately that she forgot all about this stupid damn plan of hers about marrying a millionaire.

And do what? Marry you instead?

He shook his head. Where had that come from? Then realised that Amber was looking at him worriedly.

'Have I done it wrong again?' she asked.

'No, that's fine,' he told her. 'Top marks!'

'Great,' she said, grinning. 'I'd have hated to mess up tomorrow and have everyone think I'm stupid.'

Whereas it didn't matter what he thought. Not that he thought she was stupid, far from it. But it hurt to realise his opinion was of no importance. He wasn't sure why. Pride, perhaps. He wasn't interested in a woman who wanted to marry for money, no matter how good her reasons were. He'd been down that path before.

He picked up his own lifejacket and quickly slipped it on, aware that she was watching him.

'It's really kind of you to take me under your wing like this, you know,' she said. 'Not many people would do it. Why are you?'

A good question.

He shrugged his shoulders. 'I guess I'm just a kind-hearted soul who likes to help out a damsel in distress.'

'Even a mercenary one?'

It was direct question and he knew she wanted a direct answer.

'I don't think you're mercenary,' he said, slowly. 'But I do think you're being foolish. OK, marrying Randy will get your parents out of a hole but what about you? You'll be in a loveless marriage.'

'Yeah, well, I'm done with love,' she said bitterly and he was shocked to see the pain in her eyes. 'So I'm prepared to settle with helping my folks out. And who knows, maybe me and Randy – if he does ask me to marry him – will make a go of it.'

'He, needs an heir. That's one of the conditions of his inheritance,' Jed reminded her. His gaze held hers. 'Are you prepared for that?'

'I'm not totally naïve,' she said. 'Of course I know that Randy will want ... er ... a physical relationship. I can handle it,' she retorted.

She turned away and walked over to the rails. 'The sea's lovely and calm today, isn't it?

He could take a hint. She wanted to change the subject, and who could blame her. He had no right to question her like that. But he liked her and didn't want to see her hurt and he knew that Randy and his friends would chew her up and spit her out. She wasn't tough enough for them. Not like her friend, Callie. *It's her problem, not yours,* he reminded himself. The sooner this trip was over the better. He was beginning to think it had been a dumb idea to ask her to accompany him. He could do with putting distance between himself and Amber, not spending more time with her.

They'd been sailing for half an hour when Amber felt the first feelings of nausea in the pit of her stomach. She rested her back against it and took a deep breath.

'Move to the centre of the boat and focus on the horizon, looking at the sea makes it worse,' Jed told her.

She nodded and took a few wobbly steps forward, almost losing her balance. In a flash, Jed was besides her, taking her arm, guiding her to the nearest deck chair.

'I'm so sorry,' she said, clutching his arm, 'I guess this means I do suffer from sea sickness.'

She sat down on the chair and buried her face in her hands. She felt awful. She would be mortified if this happened when she was on the boat with Randy and the others tomorrow.

'Here, try and eat these, they'll make you feel better. I promise.' Jed passed her a couple of dry crackers. 'I'll go and make you some ginger tea.'

Amber tentatively nibbled on one of the crackers. Yuk, it was salty! The thought of actually being sick horrified her though, so she forced herself to chew it. And by the time Jed returned with a cup of ginger tea and some sliced apple she'd managed to eat one of the crackers.

'Well done, now see if you can eat these apples. The combination of the salt in the crackers and acid in the apple helps calm your stomach.'

'I hope you're right,' she said as another wave of nausea swept over her.

She nibbled the apple slices and sipped the ginger ale.

By the time she'd finished them she felt slightly better, although she still didn't feel capable of moving. The nausea had subsided a little but her head was swimming dizzily.

'Here we are, put this on your wrist,' Jed was kneeling besides her. He took his hand in hers and a new kind of dizziness raced through her body. How could she react to him like that when she felt so ill? She looked down to see him slip a grey, stretchy band onto her wrist. 'What is it?'

'A travel band,' he told her. 'They're quite effective on some people. Let's hope you're one of them.'

'How do they work?' she asked, partly because she really wanted to know and partly because he was still holding her hand and she trying not to think just how much she liked it.

'Those white buttons on the inside of the band press on your acupuncture points and are supposed to stop the queasiness,' he explained, releasing her hand. 'If they don't work there's another couple of cures we can try.'

'I think I'd better back out of going sailing with Randy tomorrow,' she decided. 'I couldn't cope with another day like this. I feel awful'

'You'll be fine,' Jed reassured her. 'Now we know you suffer from sea sickness we can give you some medication before you go. If you wear these bands as well then you should keep the nausea at bay. Anyway, the more you sail, the more you'll get used to it.'

Amber wasn't sure that bobbing about on the sea was something she wanted to get used to. She much preferred travelling on firm land and the journey seemed to be taking forever. 'How much longer before we get there?' she asked.

'About an hour,' he informed her.

Great, another hour of feeling sick, dizzy, and totally yukky. Why was she doing this?

To try and stop your parents losing their ancestral

home because of that rat you got engaged to, that's why, she reminded herself. *Now stop whinging and remember what Jed said, focus on the horizon and thank your lucky stars that the sea is calm, otherwise you'd find out just how bad sea sickness can be!*

After a while, she did start to feel better. Well, enough to stand at the rail and look out over the sea, watching the different birds soar overhead, squawking and cawing.

'I never seen some of these birds before,' she said. 'Do you know the names of them all?'

'Most of them,' Jed replied. 'That one's a razorbill.' He pointed to a black and white bird flying overhead. 'See the white band near the tip of its black bill?'

'What about that one?' A grey and white bird was perched cheekily on the railings at the front of the yacht. 'I think it's hitching a ride.'

'That's a northern fulmar,' he said. 'And this one flying overhead is a kittiwake. See its red legs? There are black-legged kittiwakes too.'

Amber listened, fascinated as Jed told her a bit about the birds and their habitats. He was obviously a real authority on birds, yet he had a way of talking about them that brought their characters alive without being in the least boring.

'How have you had time to study birds so much?' she asked. 'I thought your job would be really demanding.'

'It is but I get time off to. It isn't all hard work.'

She wanted to question him more, find out how long he'd been working for his boss and what line of business he was in but sensed that he didn't like to talk about it. He sort of closed up every time she mentioned his work. *He's probably scared that I'm after his millionaire boss*, she thought.

'We're nearly there. That's Blyte Island,' Jed said as a small craggy island came into view.

Amber peered at it, fascinated. As they got nearer she

saw huge cliffs jutting up on each side of the island, guarding it like a fortress. It looked so wild, formidable, and deserted that she could well believe the scores of sea birds squawking as they flew to and from the cliffs were the only inhabitants. In fact, it appeared inaccessible, as there was no sign of any beach. The island seemed completely surrounded by cliffs. How did they get onto it? She peered closer for a sign of any gap in the cliffs but they looked impenetrable.

'We'll have to drop the anchor and go over to the island in the dinghy,' Jed said, seeing her puzzled look and guessing the reason for it. 'Apparently, there's a small landing beach over on the left side.'

'Apparently? Does that mean you've never been here before?' Amber asked him.

'Nope.' He grinned. 'But don't worry, I've done my research. I contacted the warden, Mike Swinton, a few days ago asking permission to visit the island and he filled me in on the procedure.'

She watched as Jed dropped the sails, switched on the engine, and took over the wheel so he could guide the yacht closer. *He's so strong and capable*, she thought. She bet he could turn his hand to anything.

As they got nearer to the island they saw some large buoys bobbing up and down in the sea.

'Those are the landing buoys,' Jed said, pointing. 'We have to drop our anchor in the specially designated landing bay so we don't damage the wildlife on the sea bed. The whole area, including the marine life, is a nature reserve.'

'I can see why, it's beautiful.' Amber gazed at the sun-kissed yellow granite cliffs in awe 'So wild and untamed.'

'It's that all right. Apart from the warden and occasional visitor the only other life here are the animals and birds.'

Amber wanted to ask more questions but Jed was busy dropping anchor then releasing the dinghy, which thankfully had an outboard motor, into the sea. Shortly afterwards they were both aboard the dinghy, heading towards the small landing beach, leaving the yacht securely tied to one of the buoys.

Sure enough, to the left of the island they saw a small bay with a narrow stretch of sand. 'There we are, what did I tell you?' Jed said. 'You'll soon be on dry land again.'

It will be relief to feel solid ground beneath my feet again, Amber thought as they chugged through the sea. But she wouldn't have missed this trip for anything. Jed was good company and the island was beautiful. She couldn't wait to explore it.

When they got as close as they could to the beach, Jed moored the dinghy then they both got out and paddled through the shallow sea. Amber felt a tinge of excitement as she stepped onto the small stretch of golden sand and gazed up at the imposing cliffs. It was as if time had stood still and the twenty-first century hadn't touched the island. *Maybe not the twentieth or nineteenth either,* she thought with a grin. She bet the warden didn't have many mod cons.

The air echoed with the sounds of birds, flying, squawking, chirping. They were everywhere. Amber recognised a couple of puffins nesting on a cliff, birds she'd only ever seen on TV or in books, and understood why this was a nature reserve. Some of these birds were probably quite rare and had to be protected.

Then she realised Jed was watching her in undisguised amusement, his arms folded across his chest.

'Like it?' he asked.

'I love it!' She waved her hand in a sweeping gesture to encompass her surroundings. 'It's incredible.'

'I hope you're just as enthusiastic after the climb.'

She stared at him. 'Climb? What climb?'

'Well, in case you hadn't noticed this is a rather small beach. The rest of the island is up there.' He pointed to the top of the very steep cliffs.

She swallowed as she gazed up at the cliffs.

'They're ... high ...'

'Over three hundred feet in some places,' he agreed.

'That high?' She gulped, scanning the cliffs for jutting out rocks they could use as footholds. She could make out a few but they were scattered here and there. And if you slipped there was a sheer drop to the beach below. She looked at Jed but his expression was impassive. Was he serious?

'I don't suppose you've got rock-climbing equipment on you, have you?' she asked. She was sure she'd have noticed if Jed had been carrying rope, pick-axes, and the other paraphernalia rock climbers had to take with them to ensure that they stayed alive. Mind you, that huge rucksack he'd brought with him could hold anything ...

'Nope, but then we don't need it ...'

'What!' She gasped incredulously. 'Are you seriously suggesting that we try climbing those cliffs without rope, protective hats or anything?' Not that she'd attempt to climb them with those things anyway, but there was no need for him to know just how scared she was.

'Well, you can go up that way if you want. I'll take the easier route.'

He was openly laughing at her now. Damn him! So they didn't have to climb the cliffs after all. She looked around again, but couldn't see any steps. 'What route is that?' she asked.

He picked up the heavy rucksack as if it was feather light, put it on his back, then pointed over to the cliff at the left of them. 'That way. There's a path going up the rocks. Or so I've been told,' he said. 'Let's see if we can find it.'

Amber followed him and as they got nearer to the cliff she saw to her relief that it wasn't so steep on this side and there was some sort of rugged path running up it. It still looked too precarious for her peace of mind, although she was relieved to see that a slip would send her plunging into a rough gorse bush rather than to her death. Thankfully, she'd had the presence of mind to wear trainers with a fairly good grip and her shorts. There's no way she could have attempted this path in the sundress and sandals Callie tried to persuade her to wear, saying she should look her best at all times because she never knew who she'd bump into. Mind you, she wished she'd brought a small rucksack she could carry on her back. It was going to be difficult to climb with this shoulder bag. She decided to wear it diagonally across her chest, like she used to do with her school bag, so put the strap over her head and rested the bag under her right arm. There, that was more secure.

Jed watched her, thoughtfully. 'Think you can manage it?' he asked. 'According to the warden it's a safe route and takes about fifteen minutes to get to the top.'

She nodded. 'Well if the warden says it's safe that's fine by me.'

'Let's go then.'

He started up the path and she followed him, willing herself not to look down. Although she wasn't exactly scared of heights, she didn't think she could cope with the view down until she was safely at the top. Jed seemed to sense this, as he kept turning around to check she was OK and, on more than one occasion, stopped to help her up a particularly difficult part. Something she was quite sure Randy would never have done. In fact, she couldn't imagine Randy coming to an island like this to photograph rare birds. Randy, although only a couple of years younger than Jed, struck her as immature, a good time guy whereas Jed was more thoughtful and caring. The sort of guy you could lean on in a crisis.

Whoa, what was she doing thinking of Jed like that? *He's just a friend*, she reminded herself, even if he did make her heart flutter a bit – which was hardly surprising. Any red-blooded woman would respond the same way –he was an incredibly sexy bloke. In fact, if you had a sexual magnetism scale he'd go right off the top of it, whereas Randy would be hovering somewhere near the middle – there was no way his bland good looks and little boy charm could compete with Jed's all- male sex appeal.

'Oww!' She stumbled on a rock, slipped, and screamed as she started to slide down the cliff but Jed grabbed her and pulled her back up.

'Don't panic, I've got you!' He hauled her up so she was standing on the narrow path besides him. 'Are you OK?' His voice was soft, gentle, full of concern.

'Thanks.' She took a deep breath to calm herself down. She should have been concentrating on climbing up the steep and rocky cliff path, not thinking about Jed. And now he was looking at her with those gorgeous eyes of his and her heart was fluttering again, but this time it wasn't with fright. 'I'm fine, honest.'

'OK, well, maybe you should go in front,' he suggested. 'At least that way I can keep an eye on you.'

'Big mistake to tell her to walk in front, Jed' he thought as Amber walked up the cliff path ahead of him in her tight white shorts. The sight of her lovely, shapely legs sent goose bumps down his spine and what was even more arousing was he knew she wasn't aware of the effect she had on him. He'd met women who pouted, wriggled seductively, and batted their eyelashes all the time, fully aware of the effect it had on men and quite prepared to use it to their advantage. But Amber was completely guileless. With him she was totally natural and at ease and he hated to think how mixing with Randy and his rich set would change her. Hated to think of her beautiful, sweet, innocent face becoming hard and false, of her learning to scheme and manipulate, using people for her own ends. It's her life. *Her decision to marry for money, leave her to it.*

That's what I should have done in the first place, he thought grimly. There was no need for him to get involved. He'd only met the woman a couple of days ago and already she was intruding on his thoughts far more than he was comfortable with. Whatever had possessed him to invite her along today just so she could get a bit of sailing experience and impress that creep Randy and his no good friends? It wasn't his problem if she was too innocent for them, too naïve, too sincere. He should have left her to it. And that's exactly what he was going to do as soon as they got back that evening. Tomorrow she could go sailing with Randy and when she returned he'd be gone, on his way back to America. Then he could get on with his life and forget she ever existed.

Chapter Four

Rule number 4: Act cool and let him do the running

'We're here!' Amber yelled enthusiastically. 'We're at the top and – Oh, Jed, it's beautiful!'

Jed stepped up onto the cliff besides her, smiling at the rapture on her face as she gazed around at the wild, untamed landscape. She was right, it was beautiful. Rugged terrain stretched out in front of them, partly covered in long grass from which the occasional riot of colour heralded the welcome intrusion of a bunch of wild flowers. Birds flew overheard while others nested on the nearby cliffs. His experienced eye quickly spotted herring gulls, skylarks, and water pipits and he itched to take his camera from out of his rucksack and start capturing it all on film. But he stopped himself. It was best to see the warden first, find out what areas, if any, were out of bounds. Then he could take all the photos he wanted.

'It certainly is,' he agreed. 'Let's introduce ourselves to the warden then we can have a look around. That's his house over there.' He pointed to a stone cottage in the distance. 'With a bit of luck he'll be in.'

They walked over to the cottage in companionable silence. Amber was constantly looking around, her face enthralled as if she was entranced by it all. Which surprised Jed, as he would have thought a city girl like her would find a remote, uninhabited island a bit boring. He found it far from boring. He almost envied the warden living here, away from the pressures of the world, no business deals to negotiate, no targets to meet, no wheeling and dealing. Just living in peace and tranquillity, looking after the animals and birds. It seemed idyllic. But he was realistic enough to realise that living in a place like this would have its own problems. Isolation, the battle with the elements, the longing for human company to mention just a few.

'Is he married?' Amber asked.

'Sorry?' Jed dragged himself out of his thoughts to look at her.

'I was wondering if the warden was married. It's beautiful here but it must be lonely for him with no one to talk to.'

'I've no idea but I shouldn't think so. I can't imagine any woman being happy enough to live here,' Jed replied. 'No shops, no neighbours …'

'I don't know. If you were with the man you loved that wouldn't matter, would it? Just the two of you on this island,' she sighed wistfully. 'It's tempting, though I guess I'd miss people after a while.'

'I'm sure you would,' Jed said dryly. 'Not to mention shops, clubs, the theatre and parties.'

'Probably' she admitted. 'But it would be lovely to have a holiday home over here so you could come and chill out whenever the pressure of life got too much for you.'

'Well, if you marry someone rich enough you can buy your own island and fly over whenever you feel like a bit of solitude. I'm not sure that Randy's in that league though. Maybe you ought to set your cap higher.' The words were out before he could stop them and he could see by her face that they'd hit home.

Her face clouded over and her eyes looked troubled. 'I guess you have a pretty low opinion of me. I know I must seem like a gold-digger to you but I have to do this. Besides,' she said defensively, 'I'm not hurting anyone.'

He shrugged. 'It's your life.'

Why should he care? He pushed away the tempting

thought of living in the quaint stone cottage with Amber which had crept uninvited into his mind and strode purposefully on. The sooner this day was over the better.

Jed could hear a dog barking as they approached the cottage.

'A dog must be good company on a remote island like this,' Amber said as they waited for the warden to open the door. 'Everyone needs something to come home to. It's a wonderful place for a dog to be, too. No traffic or neighbours to worry about, free to roam wherever it wants.'

'Well, it seems like the dog hasn't been left free to roam today,' Jed said, when a few minutes had passed and there was still no sign of the warden despite the dog's loud barking. 'Mike must be out. I've got his mobile number so I'll give him a ring, let him know we've arrived and check if any area is out of bounds. I don't want to go anywhere I shouldn't.'

Amber watched as Jed took his mobile phone out of his pocket, flipped it open and phoned the warden.

'I can't get through. Either he's somewhere he can't get a signal or his battery's dead.'

She could hear the dog whining pitifully on the other side of the door and felt instinctively that something was wrong.

'That isn't a normal bark. The dog sounds upset about something,' she said. 'And why would the warden leave a dog locked inside on such a lovely day? Surely he'd take it with him or leave it out to roam around?'

Jed slipped his phone back in his pocket. 'You could be right. Maybe we should check that inside. Mike could be lying injured or something. It's best to be on the safe side.' He reached for the door handle and turned it. 'Just as I thought, unlocked. I guess there's no reason to lock your door when you live on a remote island like this.'

As soon as Jed opened the door, the dog's barking got more frantic. Amber stepped back nervously.

'Maybe this isn't such a good idea, after all,' she said. 'That dog could think we're breaking in and go for us.'

'We'll just open it a fraction and shout to see if Mike's there.' Jed pushed the door open a little further and called out.

'Mike! Are you there?'

Immediately, a black nose wriggled through the gap and its doggy owner barked and whined as it tried to get out.

'Give it enough room to put its head out so we can reassure it,' Jed said.

He opened the door further and the head of a black and white border collie appeared through the opening. The dog looked more worried than threatening and Amber immediately felt sorry for it. She patted it gently on the head to reassure it.

'Hello. Who are you then?' she asked softly.

The dog immediately quietened down. It wriggled its head and shoulders through the opening and nudged Amber's hand with its head.

'Oh look, isn't it sweet?' Amber said.

'I think we're quite safe, it's definitely not a guard dog,' Jed said, smiling. He pushed the door wide open. 'Mike! Are you there?'

The dog ambled out and Amber saw at once that it was heavily pregnant.

'Oh, poor thing, it looks like it's about to have pups any minute,' Amber said, bending down to stroke the dog. 'Perhaps that's why the warden left it behind?'

'You're probably right,' Jed said. 'He's obviously not in and we've no right intruding like this and unsettling the dog in its condition. I'll put a note through the door to let him know we've arrived and we'll take a look around.'

The dog fixed its gaze on Amber, barked, then walked

back inside the cottage, stopping to turn and bark again, before heading off down the hall.

'It wants us to follow,' Amber said. 'Something's wrong, Jed!'

As if it heard, the dog turned around and barked even louder.

'I think you're right!' Jed pushed the door wide open and stepped in.

Amber was close on his heels as he followed the dog down the hall, through the lounge and into a bedroom. Jed paused for a mere nanosecond at the bedroom door and Amber caught him up. She glanced over his shoulder and saw a man, writhing in agony in the bed. The dog was sitting beside him, one paw on the duvet. It barked at Jed and Amber, as if asking them to help. The man feebly raised his hand to place it on the dog's head and muttered something.

'Mike!' Jed covered the room with long, urgent strides and knelt down by the bed. 'It's Jed. Jed Curtess. Can you tell me what's wrong?' He held the man's wrist and expertly took his pulse.

'Appendix, I think.' The warden's voice was little more than a whisper. The sweat was dripping off his face, and it was obvious he was in severe pain.

Amber knelt down on the other side of the bed, a knot of worry forming in her stomach. She knew that a burst appendix was fatal if it wasn't treated quickly. So, apparently, did Jed. He was already dialling the emergency services on his mobile phone.

'Air ambulance, please,' he said briskly. 'It's an emergency.'

The man was sweating profusely. Amber hurried to the bathroom, grabbed a towel, put it under the cold water tap, wrung it out, then took it back to the bedroom, placing it over his forehead. Mike mouthed his thanks, his eyes etched with pain.

She squeezed his hand. 'You'll be OK,' she told him.

Jed had now finished his call. 'The Air Ambulance is on his way,' he said, bending down by the bed so Mike could hear him. 'They'll soon have you in hospital. Just hang in there a bit longer.'

'Thanks.' The word was little more than a whisper. A spasm of pain crossed his face and he shut his eyes.

The dog sat patiently at the side of the bed, resting its chin on the bedclothes and watching Mike with soulful eyes. Amber patted the dog gently on the head. 'He'll be OK, girl,' she said, softly.

Why hadn't Mike phoned for help himself as soon as the pain got bad? He'd obviously guessed what was wrong with him, so he must have had first aid training. Then she spotted the mobile phone by his pillow and, picking it up, saw that the screen was blank. So that was it, he'd forgotten – or been too ill – to charge it up.

Mike opened his eyes again and looked at Amber. 'Tess,' he gasped. 'Can't leave Tess. Pups due any time. Phone ... relief warden.'

The dog pricked up its ears at the sound of its name.

'Don't worry, we'll look after Tess until another warden arrives,' Amber assured him.

'Promise.'

She could see the effort it cost him to speak. 'I promise.'

His eyelids flickered then closed.

Tears pricked Amber's eyes. Mike was in so much pain yet his first thought had been for his dog. She blinked as her eyes filled. What if he had died? Then she felt a hand on her shoulder, warm and comforting.

'He'll make it,' Jed said, softly.

Amber looked up at him, her eyelashes wet. 'He looks so ill.'

'If the appendix has burst, peritonitis could have set in and there's bound to be bacterial infection,' Jed told her.

'That's probably what's giving him a fever.'

'And how long before ...' She couldn't bring herself to say the words.

'A few hours if left untreated. But don't worry, he'll soon be in hospital. He'll be fine.'

Fortunately, the helicopter arrived in record time. It landed as near to the cottage as possible and Jed went out to meet the medics. Amber shut Tess in the kitchen thinking it might be too upsetting for the little dog to watch its master being taken away.

'Stay there and be a good girl, Tess. I'll come and let you out again soon,' she said, softly.

Jed returned with the doctor, who quickly checked Mike over. He confirmed the appendix had burst and that peritonitis had set in.

'You found him in good time, but we need to get him to hospital fast,' he said.

Taking his mobile phone out of his pocket, he phoned the hospital to warn them a patient was coming in who needed an operation. Then he and Jed gently placed Mike on a stretcher, strapped him in, and carried him into the helicopter.

'I hope he'll be OK,' Amber said as the helicopter took off.

Jed placed his arm around her shoulder. 'You heard what the doctor said, we found him in time. He's got every chance of making a full recovery.'

'What if we'd arrived a bit later?' Tears welled up in her eyes and she wiped them away with the back of her hand. 'Mike would have died all alone, and in pain.'

Jed pulled her to him, encasing her in his arms. He lowered his head and kissed her gently on the forehead. 'But we didn't arrive too late, sweetheart. He's on his way to hospital and he's going to be fine.'

Then, Amber remembered her promise. 'Jed, I promised him we'd look after Tess until a relief warden arrived.'

'I know. I'll phone the Trust now and arrange for one to come over. They'll probably be here by the time I've finished taking the photographs for my article.'

He released her and started walking back to the cottage. Amber stared after him, almost in a daze, her senses reeling.

Sweetheart.

The word echoed in her mind. It sounded so ... loving. And the way he'd held her, the touch of his lips on her forehead ...

He was comforting you, Amber, that's all. Jed's like that. Kind and caring.

And incredibly sexy.

Not that she was attracted to him. Of course not.

She pulled herself together and followed him into the cottage, going straight to the kitchen to let Tess out. The poor dog was agitated, so Amber calmed her down then looked around for Jed. She could hear him on the phone. Following the sound of his voice, she found him in a small room, which Mike obviously used as an office.

From what she could gather from the one-sided conversation, the Trust couldn't send a warden straight away. She frowned. What were they going to do? She'd promised Mike they would stay and look after Tess until the relief warden arrived. She looked down at the dog, who had followed her into the office and was now lying dolefully by her feet.

'I guess you're wondering what's going on, eh, Tess?' she said, kneeling down and stroking the dog's silky head. 'Well, don't worry, we won't leave you on your own.'

'I'm afraid that they can't send a warden until tomorrow morning,' Jed told her when he'd finished his phone call.

Amber got to her feet, chewing her bottom lip worriedly. 'But I promised Mike we'd look after Tess. We can't leave her on the island by herself – not in her condition.'

'Maybe we can take her home with us and bring her back tomorrow?' Jed suggested.

'I'm not sure that would be wise. It might upset her,' Amber said doubtfully. 'I'm sure she hasn't got long before the pups are due and it's quite a long boat trip. Her master going away then being taken to new surroundings might be too much for her.' She looked around for the dog, but it had suddenly disappeared. 'Where's Tess?'

'She just went out, maybe she wants a drink,' Jed replied.

'I'd better check on her.' As she walked down the hall, Amber heard a noise coming from a room on her left. She peered in and saw that it was a small store-room. A big box was in the corner of the room and Tess was raking at the bottom of it, ripping paper by the sound of it. Amber crept, not wanting to alarm her. A pile of newspaper had been placed on the bottom of the box and the dog was now busy ripping it up, obviously preparing the bed for her puppies. Amber watched for a moment as the border collie circled the box, then went back to ripping up the paper again. Well, that settled it. Tess was getting ready to have the pups. There was no way they could take her home with them now.

Suddenly exhausted, the dog flopped down in the box and started panting. Amber sat down on the floor besides her, stretching her legs out in front of her, and let the little dog rest its head on her lap while she stroked it gently.

'Don't worry, girl. It'll be OK. I'm here with you,' she whispered.

'How's Tess?'

She glanced up to see Jed standing in the doorway. 'She's been making her nest. She could have the pups any time.'

'Then we must stay with her, no question of that. Have

you ever played midwife before?'

'Yes. When I was a kid our dog, Bella, had pups and Dad let me help deliver them. I think I can still remember what to do. How about you?'

'Never actually had to help out, but I've seen enough vet programmes. I reckon we can manage it between us.'

She nodded. 'Tess'll do most of the work herself. We just need to be there in case she gets tired or there are complications.'

'It seems like we're doggy-sitting for the night, then,' Jed said. 'I hope you hadn't made plans for this evening.'

'No, but I am supposed to be going sailing with Randy tomorrow and he's leaving quite early,' Amber replied. 'But there's no way I'm breaking my promise and leaving Tess.' It suddenly occurred to her that Jed might have plans for the evening. She'd promised Mike they'd look after Tess without stopping to consider what Jed wanted. 'What about you? Have you got plans for tonight?'

He shrugged. 'Nothing that can't be put on hold. If you're willing to stay and look after Tess so am I. In fact, it would be quite useful for me to spend a little longer here, get some more information and photos.'

'OK, well, I'll just phone Callie and tell her. What time shall I say we'll be home? Maybe Randy will wait for me.'

'The Trust said the warden will be over by nine so, weather permitting, I'll be able to get you back before lunch. But I should think that Randy's setting off before then. It's not much of a day's sail if you don't leave until lunchtime.'

Amber shrugged. 'Then I'll have to give it a miss.'

She eased the dog off her lap and stood up. 'Now where did I leave my bag?'

'Probably in Mike's bedroom,' Jed guessed.

He was right. She remembered putting it on the floor by Mike's bed. She went to get it, took out her mobile phone, and dialled Callie.

'You must be mad,' Callie retorted when Amber explained. 'You can't miss an opportunity like this! Randy will think you're not interested in him.'

'Tess is due to have pups anytime,' Amber reminded her. 'We can't abandon her. I'm sure Randy will understand if I explain.'

'Understand what? That you're ditching him to spend the night on a remote island with Jed looking after a stranger's dog?'

'It's not like that ...'

'That's how Randy will see it,' Callie retorted. 'Why can't you bring the dog home with you? It must be used to sailing in the warden's boat.'

'Because the upheaval and journey could upset her too much, her pups are due anytime,' Amber sighed. 'I promised Mike I'd look after Tess and that's what I intend to do. So, can you please explain to Randy? If I had his mobile number I'd phone him myself.'

'It's probably a good job you haven't because there's no reasonable way you can explain this.'

Amber suddenly had a flash of inspiration. 'Isn't rule number four to play it cool? You know, millionaires are used to being chased after so let them do the running for once? Well, that's what I'm doing, isn't it?'

'True,' Callie conceded. 'But you haven't got much time to play games. You need to get Randy interested enough to want to see you when you go back home.' She was silent for a moment. 'Mind you, it might work. Leave it to me. Oh, and Amber ...'

'Yes?'

'Get back home as soon as you can and remember, Randy's the one you're after, not Jed.'

Amber fought back a retort, aware that Jed was listening. 'I have no intention of forgetting that,' she said.

Jed raised an eyebrow as Amber ended the call. 'So this is part of your plan to hook him, is it? Looking after Tess gives you a good reason not to turn up for your sailing date and make him even more eager to see you?'

Did he really think she was that shallow?

'Of course not,' she denied hotly. 'I just said that to appease Callie because she was mad with me. I didn't even think of the rules when I agreed to look after Tess. I didn't know the warden wouldn't arrive until tomorrow, and I can't leave Tess when she's ready to give birth any minute, can I?'

'No, I know.' His voice softened a little. 'Sorry, it just seems so cold-blooded, planning to marry someone for their money.'

Yes, it was. Cold-blooded but necessary. She sighed. How could she expect him to understand?

'Does that mean you won't help me?' she asked, wondering if he'd changed his mind.

'Nope, like you I don't go back on my word,' he replied. 'Though it doesn't look like the sailing's going to come in useful now. Is there anything else you need brushing up on?'

'Dancing,' she suggested, remembering how unimpressed Randy had been with her dancing skills last night.

'OK, we'll do some dancing practice tonight. Mike's bound to have some CDs or at least a radio we can dance to.'

Amber felt a frisson of trepidation. She had thought of them practising dancing at somewhere not quite as intimate as the stone cottage. Somewhere with more people around, where she wouldn't be so aware of Jed's raw magnetism.

Grow up, Amber. Surely, at your age you can practice dancing with a man without going all weak-kneed. Honestly, it's no big deal.

'How long do you think it will be before we can phone up and see how Mike is?' she asked, anxious both for news of the warden and to change the subject.

'The doctor said the operation will take at least a couple of hours. So it's best to leave it until after lunch,' replied Jed.

Lunch. That reminded Amber how hungry she was. She hadn't eaten since the bowl of muesli she'd had for breakfast – apart from the crackers and apple on the boat, of course.

'You're not still feeling queasy, are you?' Jed asked.

She'd forgotten all about her travel sickness. It seemed ages since she was on the boat feeling like her stomach was turning inside out!

'No, just starving!'

'Good. Then how about we have a cup of coffee and something to eat? We could eat outside. I noticed a wooden table and some benches at the back of the cottage.'

Good idea,' she agreed. 'I'll go and make it and find some plates for our sandwiches – unless you want to eat out of your lunchbox?' They'd both brought a packed lunch with them.

'Eating out the lunchbox will be fine for me,' Jed said. 'Why dirty the dishes?'

Amber smiled at him and went into the kitchen to make the coffee. There was only instant but she was pleased to see that it was one of her favourite brands.

'Milk and sugar?' she asked as Jed came into the kitchen.

'I'll add my own,' he told her, opening the fridge to get the milk.

They both took their mug of coffee and lunchboxes outside to the wooden table, which had a bench joined to each side.

'I'm sure Tess will have the puppies today. She's made her nest and now she's gone quiet, as if she's conserving her strength.' Amber said. She sat down on the end of the nearest bench and placing the coffee on the table in front of her.

Jed sat opposite her. 'Tell me about your dog.'

So she told him about how she'd longed for a dog so her parents had bought her Bella for a Christmas present when she was eight. And how she and the dog had soon become inseparable.

'It sounds like you had a happy childhood.'

She nodded. 'I did. My parents married in their late thirties and thought they would never have children. Then I came along. They idolised me. Even though they were busy, Dad with his business and Mum being his secretary, they always made time for me. They always made my friends welcome. Boyfriends too', she added. 'When I got engaged to Rod they welcomed him with open arms, accepted him as one of the family. That's why it was so easy for him to con them. They trusted him because they trusted my judgement.' She couldn't keep the bitterness out of her voice. 'And now they've lost everything.'

Jed reached out and covered her hand with his. It was a workman's hand, she noticed. The hand of a man who grafted for a living. Strong yet comforting. 'Did you advise your father to buy the shares?'

The emotional memories were making her feel shaky. Or was it the feel of his hand on hers? 'Of course not, I don't know anything about shares. I didn't even know Rod had given him any financial advice. None of them told me about it.'

'Then how can it be your fault?'

'Rod was my fiancé.'

'And that makes you responsible for his actions?' Jed asked, taking his hand away and picking up his coffee mug. He sipped it thoughtfully for a moment.

Could a hand feel lonely? Because that's how hers felt without his hand covering it. She wanted to beg him to put it back. 'No, but I'm responsible for introducing him to my parents. It's because of me they trusted him.'

Jed put his mug down, a solemn look on his face.

'My mom was half Cherokee,' he told her. 'They're a proud race. She was brought up to work hard and honour her family. When she got accepted at college, her parents were so proud of her. She was the first one in her family to go to college.' He paused for a moment. 'She was halfway through her first year when she met a guy there who swept her off her feet. He moved in with her, they talked about marriage ... Then she found out she was pregnant with me and he legged it.'

'Oh, Jed ...'

'Legged it owing a month's rent and lots of other bill,' he continued, his voice grim. 'Mom quit college and took a job to pay off his debts. When she couldn't work any longer she went back to her parents, who refused to take her in. They couldn't forgive her for letting them down and – as they thought – ruining her life.'

Amber's heart went out to that poor woman as she listened. And to Jed too, knowing how he must have suffered as a young lad.

'A friend, Angie, took Mom in, looked after her until I was born, gave us both a roof over her head. When Angie died in a car accident a year later, Mom looked after her daughter, Chloe.' Jed was staring into the distance now and she knew by the look on his face the memories still pained him. 'Mom worked hard all her life to support me and Chloe, always feeling guilty for being a single parent, always taking the blame for my father running out on us, for bringing shame on her family. But it wasn't her fault. She did nothing wrong. She just fell in love with the wrong guy.' He focused his gaze back on her. 'That's all you did, Amber. You fell in love with the wrong guy. You're not responsible for Rod's actions.'

A lump formed in her throat and it was a couple of

minutes before she could steady her voice to reply. 'Your mum sounds like a wonderful woman,' she said. 'And maybe you're right. Maybe I'm not directly responsible for what Rod did. But because of him my parents are going to lose their home and I can't – won't – allow it to happen.'

Chapter Five

Rule number 5: Never let him see you looking anything but your best.

She stood up, desperate to get away from Jed for a while and get herself under control. 'I'd better check on Tess.'

She could feel Jed watching her every step of the way. As soon as she got inside the cottage, she leant back against the door and closed her eyes to keep the tears at bay. How she wished she had never met Rod. He had broken her heart and bankrupted her parents. But she wouldn't let him win. Somehow, she would repay her parents. And the quickest way was to marry Randy, so the sooner she got back to Coombe Bay the better.

Tess pattered along the corridor to greet her.

'Hello, girl. How are you?' Amber stroked the dog's silky fur. 'I bet you're hungry, eh? Let's see if we can find you something to eat.'

Amber went into the kitchen, the dog at her heels, and looked around. Where would Mike keep Tess's food?

Her first guess – the cupboard under the sink – proved right. She placed a few forkfuls of food in the dog's dish, knowing that it probably wouldn't want a heavy meal, and some fresh water. Tess ate the food, lapped up some of the water, then went back to her bed in the store-room. Amber sat down on the floor beside the dog, resting Tess's head on her lap.

'It'll be all right, Tess,' she said soothingly. 'We'll stay with you until the warden comes and Mike will be home soon.'

The dog looked at her with doleful eyes and whimpered quietly.

Jed stood in the doorway, watching Amber stroke Tess and whisper comforting words to her. She was so gentle and loving with the dog and didn't seem in the slightest bothered about the mess it was making on her shorts. He remembered how her eyes had welled with tears when she'd seen how ill the warden was, how he'd held her in his arms and kissed her forehead, longing to hold her tight and kiss her on the lips. And how she'd hurried inside on the verge of tears because of that rat, Rod. It had taken all his willpower not to run after her and comfort her. Damn it, she was really getting under his skin and now they were both alone on the island until tomorrow afternoon.

You've been celibate too long, Jed. No wonder you're lusting after the first gorgeous female you've come across.

Only she wasn't the first gorgeous female he'd met since Melissa, was she? Just the first one he'd been attracted to. Maybe it was his body telling him it was time to date again.

As if sensing his presence, Amber looked up.

'Poor Tess. She's probably wondering what's happened to Mike,' she said. 'Do you think the operation is over? Can we phone and see how he is?'

'That's what I came to tell you,' Jed eased off the doorway and stood upright. 'I've just phoned the hospital and they said they've successfully removed the appendix, no complications. Mike's out of the operating theatre but still asleep at the moment. Of course he'll need time to recuperate but he's going to be fine.'

'Oh, I'm so glad! Did you hear that, Tess?' Amber wrapped her arms around the dog's neck and hugged her. 'Mike's OK.' Then she looked over at Jed, her brown eyes brimming with unshed tears. 'I hate to think what might have happened to Mike – and Tess – if we hadn't arrived when we did.'

He fought down the urge to take her in his arms and kiss the tears away. His senses told him that getting involved with Amber would be dangerous. He was too attracted to her.

'Well, there's no need to worry. They'll both be fine,' he told her. 'Now, I'd better go and take some photos before it gets too late. Do you want to come?'

'No, I'll stay with Tess. I don't want to leave her alone,' Amber was still sitting on the floor with the dog's head in her lap.

'Do you want me to stay with you in case there's any complications?'

'There's no need. Tess should manage it by herself, most dogs do,' she assured him. 'I might have to burst one of the puppy sacks if she's too weak to do it, but that should be all.'

He hesitated. 'Are you sure? I don't like to go off and leave you alone.'

'I'd prefer it if you did, honestly. I'll keep an eye on Tess and make the beds up for us tonight. '

'OK, but if she starts to have the pups promise you'll phone me. I want to be here.'

'I promise.'

'I'll only be a couple of hours at the most.'

'Take as long as you need. Make sure you get all the photos you want.' Amber gently lifted the dog's head off her lap and got to her feet. 'I'll take a chair outside and sit in the sun,' she said. 'I can keep coming in to check on Tess.'

After swapping mobile numbers and making Amber promise that she would phone him the minute Tess went into labour, Jed picked up his rucksack and set off.

Amber was relieved to have a break from Jed's presence for a while. Her senses were always on edge when he was

65

around and the feeling disturbed her. Also, she wanted to check out the sleeping arrangements in the cottage. It was rather small and she was hoping that there were two bedrooms. She didn't fancy sharing a room with Jed.

A quick glance around showed, to her relief, that there was a second bedroom. It was small and sparely furnished but adequate. She opened the windows to air the bed, doing the same in Mike's room – where she decided it was best for Jed to sleep – taking the sheet off the bed and putting it straight into the washing machine, then hanging the duvet over the line to freshen up. That done, she went back to check on Tess. The dog was sleeping soundly so Amber decided to sit outside while the beds aired, leaving the door open in case Tess woke and wanted to come outside. She carried the deck chair she'd spotted at the back of the cottage earlier around to the front, where the sun was shining brightly, and settled down to relax for a while.

She felt so at peace on this idyllic island part of her wished she could live here forever and forget all about trying to get Randy to marry her. She allowed herself to daydream for a moment, to imagine that she lived in the warden's cottage with her husband and a couple of children playing outside. No worries, no pressure, just her and Jed.

Jed! She sat upright. What on earth was she doing imaging herself married to Jed! The sun must have got to her head and addled her brain. Time to check on Tess and start making the beds, my girl, she told herself sternly.

Just then, Tess trotted out laboriously, as if it was a huge effort, and made her way over to the hedge where she squatted down. Then she ambled over and rested her chin on Amber's lap.

'It'll all be over soon,' Amber comforted the dog, stroking her behind her ears. 'You go and have a rest whilst I make the beds.'

Tess followed Amber back inside the cottage and went straight to the nesting box, lying down with a big sigh. Amber left a bowl of fresh water just by the side of the nesting box, then went to make up the beds. She found some clean bed linen in the airing cupboard, made up the beds in both rooms, then took out the freshly washed bed linen from the washing machine and pegged it on the line. That done, she sat back in the deckchair and, exhausted, dozed off for a while

Amber opened her eyes to see Jed walking towards her and a warm glow enveloped her. He was back.

'Did you get the photos you wanted?' she asked.

'I got quite a few, though I think I'll go out early in the morning and get a few more,' he said. He indicated the washing blowing on the line. 'I see you've been busy.'

'I put some fresh linen on the beds. I thought you might like Mike's room and I'll take the smaller one, next door to Tess.'

That's it, spell the sleeping arrangements out for him. Not that he'd have any ideas about them sharing a room. Now if it was Randy, he'd expect it.

'Fine by me. How's Tess?'

'She's had a bit to eat and now she's resting,' Amber told him. 'I was about to check on her again.'

As they approached the store-room they heard the sound of Tess panting heavily.

'I'm no expert,' Jed said, 'but I think this might be it.'

Amber looked at the dog's strained face then placed her hand on its swollen belly. It was rock hard. 'I think you're right.'

'So what do we do now?' Jed asked, looking anxiously at Tess.

'I guess we leave her to it unless she gets into any trouble,' Amber said. 'We don't want to frighten her.'

'It could be a long haul, fancy a cup of coffee while

we're waiting?' Jed offered.

'That would be lovely. Milk but no sugar, please' Amber replied, her eyes still fixed on Tess, who was panting heavily. She was sure a pup would be born any minute.

She was right. A few minutes later the first pup was born. Tess expertly bit open the bag and cleaned the pup with her tongue.

'Good girl,' Amber said encouragingly. She longed to get closer and see whether the pup was male or female but didn't dare for fear of frightening the mother dog. After all, they were basically strangers to Tess.

She heard light footsteps behind her and turned to see Jed holding two mugs of coffee. He handed one out to her and, smiling gratefully, she took it off him.

'Thank you.'

'She's managing OK?' he asked, looking over at Tess.

'So far so good. Oh, look here's another one!'

As before, Tess dealt expertly with the birth of the pup. However, by the time four pups had arrived Amber could see the little dog was getting weak.

'She must be dying for a drink. I'll see if I can get her to have one.' Amber picked up the bowl of water from the side of the box and placed it on the floor right in front of the dog.

'Here you are, Tess. Have a drink,' she coaxed.

The little dog sighed then slowly stretched her head and took a few sips. The next minute she was panting heavily again and Amber knew another pup was on the way. By the time this last pup was born, poor Tess was too exhausted to bite the bag, so Amber quickly nicked it open with her nails, hoping Tess wouldn't reject it. Fortunately, the dog weakly raised her head and started licking the tiny puppy.

Amber heard Jed walking softly across the room and her skin prickled as he knelt beside her.

'Five, eh. Not bad going. I wonder what sex they are?'

'I don't think we'd better disturb her yet to find out,' Amber said, her eyes misting over as the tiny, squirming bundles fumbled their way to the warmth of their mother's body. 'Aren't they just gorgeous?'

'Wonderful,' Jed said, placing his arm around her shoulder and squeezing it gently.

She smiled at him and their eyes locked. Her breath caught in her throat as the air between hung quiet and still. Then, slowly, his face came closer and then his lips were on hers, lightly and gently at first, then deepening in intensity. And she was returning the sweet, probing kisses with ardour.

'Wuff! Wuff!

Tess's barks brought Amber shudderingly back to earth again.

Whoa! What was she thinking of, kissing Jed like this? She pulled away, fighting down the fire that was threatening to engulf her entire body, and looked over at the dog standing in the doorway.

'I think she's trying to tell us to stop congratulating ourselves, she did all the hard work,' she said, hoping her voice sounded steadier than she felt. She didn't dare catch Jed's eye, dreading what she'd see there. He'd just given her a light kiss on the lips and she'd practically thrown herself at him! He already had a low enough opinion of her because she was planning on hooking a millionaire, now what must he think?

'So she did.' Jed's voice was light, as if nothing had happened between them. Well, it hadn't, had it? It was only a quick kiss, for goodness sake.

You call that a quick kiss?

She heard Jed get up but still didn't trust herself to turn and face him.

'I'll go and write up my notes and check through the photos I've taken.' he told her. 'I'll be in Mike's study if you need me.'

'OK.'

The next minute he was gone, leaving her to her thoughts.

Oh, nice one, Amber. Great timing to snog the guy like that when you've got to spend the whole evening together, not to mention tomorrow morning and the boat trip home.

Hang on, he kissed me.

Yes, but you didn't have to kiss him back quite so enthusiastically, did you? She cringed as she remembered the way she'd ran her fingers through his hair, pulling his head closer to her. What had come over her?

He's an attractive guy and you were emotional because of the pups. It's no big deal. Just shrug it off like nothing happened. Jed has. The kiss had obviously meant nothing to him.

She got up and brushed down her shorts, wrinkling her nose at how grubby they were. She wished she'd bought a spare pair with her, and some clean undies too. She didn't relish wearing the same clothes the next day. Maybe she could swill them through later and hang them to out to dry overnight. Until then she could at least have a wash and touch up her make up so she'd look a bit more respectable. Where had she left her bag? Oh no, the study, she realised, where Jed was working. Well, she couldn't hide away from him just because she - or to be fair, they – had got a bit carried away with a kiss. She was sure she were both adult enough to handle it.

Running her fingers through her hair in a feeble attempt to tidy it, and refusing to dwell on why she was even bothering, she walked along the hall to the study. The door was half-open. Taking a deep breath, she pushed it open further and stepped inside the room. Jed was sitting at the desk, writing in a notepad. He glanced up and smiled when she came in.

'Everything OK?' he asked.

'I came for my bag so I could freshen up a bit,' she told him. 'I can't do anything about my grubby clothes but I can at least try to look presentable.'

Jed pushed the chair back and stood up, his tall, lean frame towering above her, just a few centimetres away. Close enough to reach out and touch.

Stop it!

'I've been thinking about that, too,' he said. 'When I've phoned the hospital to check on Mike I'll go over to the boat and get some clean clothes. I can bring some for you. My boss's wife won't even miss them.'

It would be good to have a shower and change into something clean, Amber thought. If only she had some clean undies too. She certainly wasn't going to ask Jed to sort some out for her though.

'Even better, you could come with me,' he suggested. 'I'm sure you'd like to choose the clothes yourself.'

She hesitated, weighing up the ordeal of the journey down – and back up – the steep cliff path against the luxury of clean undies.

'I'll hold your hand down the cliff path if that's what's worrying you,' he offered, his eyes twinkling.

Was the guy psychic?

'Of course not, I was just wondering if Tess would be OK,' she replied.

The big grin that spread over his face told her that he knew she was lying.

'They'll be perfectly fine. In fact, they could probably do with some time alone together.' He perched on the side of the desk and folded his arms across his chest, his grin widening. 'Are you sure you it isn't the cliff path that's putting you off? Or the boat ride? It's only a few minutes to the *Chenoa,* you won't get seasick in such a short time.'

'Of course not,' she said indignantly. 'I told you I was worried about Tess, but you're right she'll be fine, so, yes I'll come with you.'

'Good.' He stood up and reached in his pocket for his mobile phone. 'I'll call the hospital first to check on Mike, then we'll get going.'

From the ensuing conversation, Amber gathered that Mike was sleeping and making satisfactory progress. Jed left a message for him that Tess had five pups and they were all doing well and promised to ring back later.

'He's fine, the nurse said he's made a full recovery but will have to stay in hospital for a couple of weeks, then he'll need a few weeks convalescence.'

'Thank goodness for that.' Amber smiled in relief. Mike was OK, so were Tess and the pups. Now all she had to do was get through the night on the island with Jed. Tomorrow they would go home. She'd hopefully meet Randy and carry on with her plan. As Callie had reminded her, it was Randy she should be spending time with, not Jed.

'Let's get going then,' Jed said. 'The sooner we set off the sooner we get back.'

She was about to nod her agreement when she remembered the reason she'd come into the study in the first place – to get her bag so she could tidy herself up a bit. Spotting it on the floor besides the desk she reached down and picked it up. 'Give me five minutes,' she said and set off for the bathroom.

Actually, going down the slope was almost as bad as going up it, and Amber would have slipped a couple of times if it wasn't for Jed reaching for her hand and holding onto her. She was quite relieved to reach the beach and feel flat land under her feet once more.

'I don't think I'd like to do that too often,' she said, trying not to let the fact that Jed was still holding her hand unnerve her.

'It's not too bad providing you take it slow.' Jed kept his grip on her hand as they walked over the sand then waded out in the sea to where the dinghy was moored. When he finally let go, she felt ridiculously bereft.

They took their lifejackets from under the seat and fastened them on – this time Amber remembered which was the front – then Jed started the engine and they set off around the island.

The *Chenoa* floated majestically in the middle of the ocean, still anchored to the buoy. *It's such a beautiful yacht*, Amber thought. *It must be fantastic to be able to afford a boat like that to sail around the world in.* Goodness knows what other luxuries Jed's boss had at home too. She wondered what he did for a living that made him so much money.

That's the sort of life she'd have if she married Randy. The thought shook her. She'd never stopped to consider how her life would change if she married a millionaire. All she'd been concerned about was helping her parents, preventing them from losing the family home. Now, as the dinghy zoomed across the sea to the elegant yacht, she stopped to think about the effects such a marriage would have on her life. She'd live in luxury, true. And probably never have to work again. But what sort of life did Randy lead? Was he just a playboy, as he seemed, intent on living solely for pleasure? If so, would he conduct affairs after they were married and she'd provided the heir that he wanted? And would she be expected to ignore them? The thought made her physically sick.

Get real, Amber, most men are like that, look at Rod. At least by marrying Randy you'll be helping your parents out, probably saving your father from another – maybe fatal – heart attack. And as her heart wouldn't be involved, Randy couldn't hurt her, could he?

'Are you OK, you look a bit pale? You're not feeling sick, are you?' Jed's voice was full of concern.

Yes, but not for the reason you think. 'No, I'm fine.' She assured him.

Jed cast her a doubtful glance but they had reached the *Chenoa* so he didn't pursue it.

Once on board, Jed told her to help herself from any clothes she needed whilst he sorted out something for himself. 'I'm going to take a quick shower. Feel free to do the same. Oh, and there's underwear and nightwear in the set of six drawers, some of it still in the packets. Find a new set and keep it.'

New underwear? That was fantastic. She hated the idea of wearing underclothes anyone else had worn – especially a stranger.

'Are you sure your boss's wife won't mind?' she asked.

'No, she won't even miss them.'

'Then I will. Thank you, you're so kind.'

He shrugged. 'It's nothing. You remember the way to the cabin, don't you?'

How could she forget? 'Yes, thanks. I won't be long,' she replied, setting off down the corridor, to the room where she'd slept the night of the party.

She stepped inside the cabin, glancing at the bed, which was now freshly-made, and walked over to the wardrobe, sliding open the doors to access the clothes inside. *I don't want anything too dressy*, she thought, searching through the array of designer dresses, tops, and trousers. Another pair of shorts or cotton trousers would do. Ah, these were perfect. She selected some cropped denims, checking the size to make sure they'd fit, and a pretty white top with scalloped edging. Now, for some underwear.

She looked around the room and saw a chest of six drawers on the far wall. That was probably where the underwear was kept.

She was right. When she opened the top drawer, she saw piles of bras and knickers, still in packets. They were a size smaller than she usually took, but she was sure she could squeeze into them. It would be worth it to have fresh underwear. Opening the other drawers, she found even more underwear, nightdresses, pyjamas, and tights. She went back to the top drawer and searched through the packets, hoping to find a sensible white bra and matching knickers. She soon realised that Jed's boss's wife didn't do sensible. Most of the underwear consisted of incredibly sexy, almost transparent, bras with matching barely-there thongs. She'd never have the nerve to wear anything like that! Amber flicked through the packets, deciding that if she couldn't find sensible, she'd have to make do with anything remotely decent.

Finally, she found a white lacy bra with a matching, delicate pair of briefs. She'd never seen anything so beautiful in her life. They seemed generously cut too, so hopefully wouldn't be too tight.

The millionaire's wife didn't do sensible nightwear either. Amber selected a black nightie that was slightly less sheer than the others in the drawer, and a matching negligee. *I'd better make sure I don't go sleep-walking and bump into Jed in the night,* she thought.

She had a quick shower, towelled, and dressed in the clean underwear, cropped jeans, and top – which thankfully fit fine – placed her clothes in a plastic bag, then in a pink holdall along with another top and pair of knickers for the next day. Finally, she selected a couple of magazines from the pile on the bedside table and set off to find Jed.

She found him in the kitchen, inspecting the fridge.

'I've taken another top and clean underwear for tomorrow and a couple of magazines, and this holdall to put them in.' She held out the bag. 'Do you want to check so you can make sure I bring everything back?'

'Of course not. I've told you, you can keep it all.' He took a container of mushrooms and some eggs out of the fridge. 'How do you fancy mushroom omelette?

Jed must have a good relationship with his boss if he has a free hand to use anything on the boat, Amber thought. She could have put anything in this holdall! Well, she didn't intend to keep it, it wouldn't be right. She'd have it all cleaned and return it as soon as she got back home.

'It sounds lovely,' she replied. 'Who's cooking, me or you?'

'I will,' he said, his eyes twinkling. 'You can do the washing up.'

'Thanks.'

'Don't mention it.' He was laughing at her. 'Now, how about a dessert? Or are you the kind of girl that never eats dessert?' He ran his eyes over her body. 'You haven't got the figure of a girl who eats dessert.'

She flushed at the admiration she saw in his gaze. 'Well, don't be fooled by appearances I'm the sort of girl who definitely eats dessert,' she replied. 'As far as I'm concerned it's the best part of the meal.'

'Right, well how does chocolate mousse grab you?'

She licked her lips at the thought. 'Wonderful!'

He grinned. 'OK, that's everything I need. Let's head back to the island and I'll cook the meal in Mike's cottage.'

Jed watched in amusement as Amber tucked into her chocolate mousse with relish, using her spoon to scrape out every last bit from the dish. 'I see you weren't joking about liking desserts.'

'Nope.'

She put her spoon in the dish and licked her lips. 'That was absolutely delicious. Where did you learn to cook like that?'

'I'm a man of hidden talents,' he quipped. 'You'd be amazed what I can do.'

She cocked her head on one side and grinned impishly. 'I wouldn't be surprised at anything you can do.'

Their gaze met and the world seemed to stand still as

her gorgeous brown eyes held and bewitched his, stirring feelings in him that he preferred to lie dormant, igniting them, fanning them into a raging flame. Then her mobile phone rang and he felt an irrational flash of irritation as she went to answer it, leaving him burning with desire.

'Randy!' The surprise in her voice was evident. 'How did you get my number?'

Jed picked up the dishes and carried them into the kitchen, trying to stamp down the wave of jealousy that was welling up inside him.

'I should be back by midday. We just have to wait for the relief warden to arrive,' Amber said.

It seemed like Randy was anxious to see her. Mind you, he couldn't blame him. If a man had to marry someone in order to gain an inheritance then Amber was a good choice. She was beautiful, kind, and fun to be with. The kind of woman anyone would want to marry.

Especially him.

Hold it right there, Curtess! Marriage isn't on your agenda. And Amber certainly won't marry someone like you. Well, not unless you told her the truth ...

And there was no way he was going to do that. The less Amber Wynters knew about him the better.

Chapter Six

Rule number 6: Don't get intimate too quickly, keep him waiting.

'Hey, I'm supposed to be washing up – you cooked, remember?' Amber walked in, her phone call evidently finished.

'You can dry instead,' Jed said. 'It's kinder to your nails. You'll never attract a millionaire with washday hands.'

She took the tea towel off the hook besides the sink, picked up a wet plate from the draining rack, and started to wipe it dry, biting her lip pensively.

'What's up? Is Randy annoyed because you're staying over on the island with me?' Jed placed a wet mug on the draining rack.

'No, he's fine about it.' She wiped the mug and placed it in the cupboard. 'In fact, he's postponed the sail until Wednesday so I can go with him.'

'You mean he's not jealous?'

'Of course not, why should he be?'

Why indeed? He wasn't any competition for a millionaire like Randy, was he?

If only they knew that Randy was nowhere near his league.

'So why the long face?'

'Randy wants me to go to a party at one of the hotels – some friends of his are getting engaged.'

'And you don't fancy going?'

'It's not that …'

He half-turned to her, his hands still in the bowl of soapy suds. 'Are we playing a guessing game or are you going to tell me?'

'Well, it's a party so they're all going to be dancing, aren't they? And you know how rubbish I am at dancing.' She flushed. 'Randy could hardly bear to dance with me last time.'

'Don't let him make you feel awkward, you danced fine with me. Anyway, I told you I'd give some extra dancing lessons,' Jed reminded her. 'When we've finished this I'll go and clear a space to dance in and find some suitable music.'

The smile she gave him illuminated her face, sending shivers down his spine. Heck, this woman sure did play havoc with his hormones.

Just a natural reaction to a beautiful woman, Jed. It's no big deal.

'Thanks, Jed. I really appreciate you helping me.'

'No problem. Can't have you showing yourself up at the party, can we?' he teased.

They finished the washing up in companionable silence. Then Amber checked on Tess and the pups while Jed went into the lounge, moved the sofa against the wall, then found a CD player and some CDs. He was kneeling on the floor flicking through them when Amber came in.

'Anything particular you want to dance to?' he asked, indicating the pile of CDs in front of him.

'I don't mind. You choose.'

'OK, it'll have to be slow and romantic. That's what all the partner dances are like.' He selected one. 'This one will do.'

He slipped the CD into the player, switched it on, then stood up and held out his arms to Amber. 'Come on, and remember, follow my lead and you'll be fine.'

As soon as she stepped into his arms Jed knew it was a mistake.

He tried to ignore the way she heightened all his senses. The lingering smell of the shower gel she'd used, the enticing feel of her soft body against his, the electrifying touch of her bare hand on his arm, the way she gnawed at her bottom lip as she concentrated on trying to follow his steps. And the desperate need he felt to hold her close and kiss those lovely lips until she begged him not to stop.

It took all his willpower but he was keeping himself under control – just – then, as if sensing his, she raised her eyes to his. He saw her pupils dilate, heard her catch her breath, felt her body tense, and, unable to stop himself, bent his head and touched her forehead with his lips. Tracing feather kisses down her face, he found her lips and possessed them, softly at first then – fuelled by her ardent response – more urgently.

His breathing quickened. Her hands caressing the back of his neck. She ran her fingers through his hair, her body pressing against him, her lips melting into his. One hand tightly around her waist, he slid the other hand up her back, pulling her closer to him.

'You're beautiful!' he murmured in her ear.

'Wuff! Wuff!'

Amber jerked her eyes open and looked around, still dazed.

'Wuff!'

Tess was standing beside her, barking at them.

Saved by the dog again! Amber thought, coming to her senses. What had possessed her to get entangled in a heavy embrace with Jed? How embarrassing.

As if sensing her change of heart, Jed released her and glanced over at the dog. 'I think Tess is trying to attract our attention,' he said lightly.

'I expect she wants to go to the toilet.' Amber tried to act cool and composed. 'I ought to feed her too. We'll have to put the dance on hold for a moment.'

'Sure. You see to Tess and I'll go and change the paper

in her bed. It must be pretty messy by now.'

Amber nodded. 'Come on, Tess.'

As soon as Amber opened the back door, the border collie trotted out, sniffing the ground and walking around in circles before going over to a far corner to relieve herself.

Amber walked over to the bench and sat down, wrapping her arms around her shoulders, hugging herself tight to stop herself shaking. She could hardly believe she had responded so passionately to Jed's kisses. Goodness knows just how carried away she'd have got if Tess hadn't interrupted them. Again.

Tess had finished her business now and came over to her, tail wagging.

'You must be my guardian angel,' she said, stroking the dog under her chin. 'That's twice you've saved me from making a complete fool of myself with Jed. I owe you big-time.'

What was the matter with her? She didn't normally get so heavy with a guy she barely knew. That might be Jed's style but it certainly wasn't hers.

OK, she was attracted to him. She couldn't deny it. And he was attracted to her too, she could tell that by the look in his eyes and the passion in the kiss they had shared, but nothing could come of it. She was going to marry a millionaire and get her parents out of the mess that slime-ball Rod had left them in. Having a torrid affair with Jed didn't fit into her plan. In fact, it was the one thing that could scupper it completely. She had to keep her distance from him, because she obviously couldn't trust herself around him. Which was extremely difficult now they were stuck on a remote island together for the whole night.

She stopped outside for a while to give herself time to regain her composure. She didn't want Jed to know just how much he disturbed her. *Is the attraction as powerful for him?* she wondered. Did he lose all control when she was around, as she did with him? Did her mere touch send his bones to quivering jelly as his did to her?

She doubted it, judging by how quickly he'd pulled himself together when Tess had disturbed them. She was sure he wanted her, but not with the same uncontrollable passion. He hadn't seemed flustered by the situation, as she had been. Was that because he was used to casual flings with women? He must meet many women – far more beautiful than she was – as he worked for a millionaire, perhaps she was just another notch on his bedpost.

Especially if he could get her to forget her plan of marrying Randy and have an affair with him instead. Choose him over a millionaire.

Her body stiffened. Is that what he was trying to do? After all, he'd made no bones about the fact that he thought she was being mercenary, yet he'd promised to help her. The two things didn't tie up. Why should he help her when he disapproved of what she was doing? Was it so he could get her to trust him, to fall for him and forget her plan? That would give his ego a real boost, wouldn't it?

But Jed isn't like that. He's kind, caring, and uncomplicated, her mind whispered. *Not scheming and devious.*

How do you know? You've only just met him. It could all be an act. Like Rod. Look how he fooled you.

'Do you fancy some hot chocolate?'

Jed was standing in the doorway.

'No thanks,' she replied.

She didn't want to sit drinking hot chocolate with him. It was too cosy and intimate. She needed to keep her distance, to avoid being alone with him. There was no way she wanted to get too close to him, to risk kissing him again. Next time she might not be saved from making a complete fool of herself.

There wasn't going to be a next time. She'd make

certain of it.

'Are you sure? I've got fresh cream.'

Drat, he sure knew her weaknesses.

'And marshmallows.'

That did it. Fresh cream she could just about resist. Marshmallows were beyond her willpower.

'Pink ones?' she asked.

'Naturally. Pink are the best.'

'OK, I'll have a cup. Thank you,' she added.

He chuckled. 'It'll be ready in five minutes.'

You're so weak-willed, Amber Wynters, she scolded herself as she walked inside.

She'd just have to make sure she remained strong-willed as far as Jed was concerned.

'I checked the sex of the puppies whilst you and Tess were outside.' Jed handed her a mug of hot chocolate with a big pink marshmallow floating on the top. 'Three girls and two boys.'

'That's fantastic.' Amber stood in the doorway. She didn't trust herself to get any closer. 'Wait till Mike knows, he'll be delighted. Do you think he'll have come around from the operation? Can we tell him?'

'Let's leave it until tomorrow, eh? It's a bit late now,' Jed replied. 'In fact, I'm just going into the study to finish a few notes then I'm turning in. I want to be up early tomorrow and take some more photos before we leave the island.'

She glanced at her watch. It was almost ten o'clock. She hadn't realised it was that late. Although she didn't usually go to bed before midnight, she suddenly felt weary. It had been a long, eventful day.

'Yeah, sure. I'll just drink this and go to bed myself.'

Amber checked on Tess, smiling at the sight of the little dog proudly feeding the tiny pups. Then she went back to the lounge and sat on the sofa, cupping her hot chocolate and mulling over the last few days' events. She felt as if her life was spiralling out of her control since she'd met Jed. She had to get him out of her head and stick to her plan to marry Randy. Especially as Randy seemed so keen on her. He'd even altered his plans so she could come sailing with him. She could hear Callie's voice in her head, *'Just follow the Millionaire Plan and you'll hook him'*.

And that's exactly what she was going to do. Now, what was rule number six?

She grabbed her bag, took out the sheet of paper she'd listed the ten rules on, and scanned it. She frowned when she spotted number five – 'Never let him see you looking anything but your best.' It's a good job she wasn't trying to hook Jed, she thought, she didn't think he'd seen her look her best yet!

Then she saw rule six and groaned as she read 'Don't get intimate too quickly. Keep him waiting'. Another rule she'd broken with Jed but she certainly wouldn't with Randy.

She'd make sure she looked her best for Randy tomorrow night. She pondered over the dresses Callie had loaned her and decided that she would either wear the long white dress or the backless red one. Both of them were sexy and stunning without being too revealing. Well, they looked that way on Callie anyway, whether they had the same effect on her was doubtful. She wore the same size clothes as Callie, but they didn't hang on her the same way. Her hips were bigger for a start, and so was her bust. Callie was so slim with long, long legs anything would look good on her.

Still, the dresses were both better than any she owned and, with a bit of luck, would detract Randy's attention from the fact that she couldn't dance. Because there was no way she was going to ask Jed for dancing lessons now – and judging by the way he'd quickly retired to the study she gathered he wasn't about to offer them.

She finished her hot chocolate and went to check on Tess again before she went to bed. She was curled up, fast asleep with the pups. Amber took a newspaper off the pile in the corner and spread it on the floor in case Tess needed the loo in the night then went to say goodnight to Jed. The study door was half-open and peering through, she could see him bent over the desk, engrossed in his work. She hesitated, wondering whether to disturb him or just go straight to bed, but, as if sensing her presence, he turned to her.

'I'm almost finished here,' he told her. 'Is everything OK?'

'Yes, Tess and the pups are sleeping and I'm off to bed now.'

His tawny eyes met hers, and she felt the familiar flutter in the pit of the stomach. 'Goodnight then.'

'Goodnight.'

Sleep eluded her.

She heard the bathroom door open and shut and, a few minutes later, the door to the bedroom next to hers – Mike's bedroom – open then shut and knew that Jed had gone to bed too. The bedsprings creak in the next room as Jed got into bed, and she had to fight down the urge to go next door and join him, take up where they'd left off before Tess had interrupted them, to feel his lips on hers again …

She groaned, burying her head in her hands, she had to take her mind off Jed before she went crazy. She switched on the bedroom lamp and looked around the room, hoping to find a book to read but there was no sign of one. She was just considering going downstairs to get a book from Mike's study when she remembered the magazines she'd borrowed from Jed's – or rather his boss's – yacht. They would do. She reached for the holdall she'd left by the bed and took one of the magazines out of it.

It was a typical upmarket glossy magazine, featuring models dressed in designer clothes, immaculate homes furnished with expensive furniture in unpractical colours such as cream and lemon, and gossipy articles about the rich and famous. *This will be my life if I marry Randy*, she thought as she browsed through it. She'd have everything she wanted and never have to worry about money again.

She'd never know love either. For she knew for certain that Randy didn't love her and probably never, and it sent a chill to her heart. She pulled herself together. So what? She'd loved Rod, hadn't she? And look where it had got her.

She flicked through the pile of magazines until her eyes felt tired and heavy. After putting them on the floor, she reached out and switched off the light then snuggled down in bed. Sleep came in bits and drabs, interrupted by jumbled up dreams of a huge wedding cake that crumbled as she tried to cut it, bank notes raining out of the sky, and dogs barking.

Dogs barking! She jerked open her eyes and realised that the barks were real. Tess must want to go out. She jumped out of bed, still half-asleep, ran across the bedroom floor, pulled open the door, ran into the hall, and collided with Jed, who was just coming out of his bedroom.

'Ouch!'

He reached out and grabbed her before she fell back on the floor, his hand gripping her arm to steady her.

'Sorry!' they both said together then laughed.

Jed reached out and flicked the light switch, and she sucked in her breath. He wore only a pair of black jersey boxer shorts that clung seductively to his hips.

Then she remembered that she was only wearing a black flimsy nightie and in this light it was probably far too revealing. She edged back into the shadows of the doorway in an attempt to preserve some of her modesty.

Jed was staring at her, his expression unfathomable. She swallowed, suddenly nervous. The air hung heavy between them, charged with tension.

'Wuff!'

Tess stood in front of them, wagging her tail, waiting patiently.

'I'll let her out.' Jed's voice was thick, as if he'd been dragged out of a sleep.

Amber nodded, not trusting herself to sleep.

For a breath-taking moment his gorgeous tawny eyes held hers, challenged her, then he turned away and set off down the hall with Tess at his heels

Amber retreated into her bedroom, shut the door, and leant against it, her body trembling. Boy, that guy certainly lit her fire!

Jed came back a few minutes later. He stopped outside the bedroom door and knocked. 'Tess is back in bed now, Amber.'

'OK. Goodnight,' she answered.

She knew he was standing outside the door, waiting to see if she would open it and talk to him but there was no way she was going to. Not with them both in such a dangerous state of undress. There was only so much self-control a girl could exert, and Jed Curtess was making her use every last iota of hers.

'Goodnight,' he replied. Then she heard him walk next door and open his bedroom door.

Mentally patting herself on the back for not giving into temptation, she climbed into bed and switched off the lamp. But it was quite a while before she got to sleep.

When she came downstairs the next morning, dressed in cropped jeans again and the spare top she'd brought with her, Amber was relieved to find a note from Jed taped to the fridge saying he'd left early to take some more photos. As far as she was concerned, the least she saw of him the better. That way she wouldn't do anything stupid like kiss him.

Honestly, she just couldn't seem to control herself when he was around.

She made a cup of frothy coffee and some toast, then cleaned out the puppies' bed, fed Tess, and let the little dog outside for a while for some fresh air and exercise. Next, she set about tidying up, ready for the relief warden to arrive. She stripped the sheet and duvet cover from the bed she'd slept in, put them in the washing machine, and went into the other bedroom to do the same to Jed's bed. Judging by the state of his bed, he'd tossed and turned most of the night, like her – though she doubted if it was for the same reasons.

The pillow still bore a slight indent where he lay. She picked it up to take off the pillowcase and caught a whiff of his potent male smell mixed with the woody cologne he wore. Slowly, almost in a dream, she sat down on the bed, hugging the pillow to her, the smell invading her senses, bringing up memories of last night, his kisses, his touch.

Her mobile beeping brought her back to earth. She took it out of her pocket and pressed the button to see who the text was from, half hoping it was Jed.

It was Randy, telling her to text him when she was on the way back and he'd meet her at the marina and take her to lunch.

He is keen, she thought. She keyed in 'Thanx. That'll be brill. C u l8tr. x Amber', and pressed send.

Time to stop daydreaming about Jed, she told herself sternly. She only had a few days left to hook Randy, and she had to make every one of them count.

She stripped the pillowcase and linen off Jed's bed, bundled them in her arms, and carried them to the washing machine, her head held high so she his scent wouldn't invade her senses again. OK, she did hold them to her cheek just once as she went put them in the machine but it was only fleetingly so it didn't count.

It had been long enough to kick in her hormones once again, though. Whatever it was that gave that guy so much sex appeal he ought to bottle it, he'd make a fortune.

She couldn't face going back into Jed's room and putting clean sheets on the bed yet, so she phoned the hospital to see how Mike was. The nurse let her speak to him, and although he sounded a bit weak, he assured her he was fine and sounded delighted to hear that Tess and the pups were doing fine. He thanked her for staying with them and she assured him it was no problem. As she finished the call, telling Mike to take care of himself, she thought wryly that she would never have guessed exactly how much a problem being in such close contact with Jed would be.

She could handle it. In a few hours they'd be back in Coombe Bay, she'd be having lunch with Randy, practising her millionaire-hooking skills on him, and she could forget all about Jed.

Forget Jed? As if!

OK, well maybe not forget, but at least she could avoid him then there'd be no chance of her falling for his potent magnetism again, would there?

Her mobile phone beeped again. She checked the message, thinking it would be Callie and her face broke into a smile when she saw it was from Jed telling her to put the coffee on because he was on his way back.

The sooner you're back at Coombe Bay, the better, Amber Wynters, she thought as she filled up the kettle. *If just a text has you grinning like an idiot you must be going soppy.*

So when Jed walked in a few minutes later, she kept her emotions completely under control as she raised her eyes from the magazine she was reading. Totally ignored how drop-dead-sexy he looked in the khaki shorts and white sleeveless vest he was wearing, she asked him calmly if he'd taken all the photos he needed.

'Yep, I've got some brilliant ones.' His eyes sparkled with enthusiasm. 'I'm really glad we came here. I'll get a few articles out of this, maybe even a book.'

'That's good. There's coffee in the pot, help yourself,' she told him and went back to reading her magazine, congratulating herself on her self-control.

It was only when Jed reached over her shoulder, turned the magazine around, and patted her soothingly on the head that she realised she'd been holding it upside down.

The relief warden, a big, friendly man called Steve, arrived just after eleven. Tess greeted him happily and it was obvious they were old friends. He explained that he often visited Mike and Tess and usually looked after the Nature Reserve when Mike went away.

'So there's no need to worry, Tess and the pups will be fine with me,' he assured them. 'And talking about pups, where are they? I want to take some photos for Mike.'

Amber took him to see the pups. She watched, smiling as he cooed over them and made a big fuss of Tess, telling her what a clever girl she was. For such a big, burly man, he was remarkably gentle with animals. She had no qualms about leaving Tess and her babies in his care.

Finally, when Steve had taken several photos and phoned the hospital to speak to Mike and assured him that he would stop until he'd fully recovered – which the doctors said would be several weeks – Amber and Jed packed their rucksacks and said goodbye.

'Sorry we have to dash off but Amber has a lunch date and I'm anxious to get started on my article,' Jed told Steve.

'Well, thank you, on Mike's behalf, for holding the fort here and looking after Tess,' Steve held out his hand. 'It's kind of you both, especially as you're both strangers to the island.'

'No problem,' Jed shook his hand.

'Goodbye, lass.' Steve offered Amber his hand.

'Bye, Steve. Give Mike our best wishes.'

They both picked up their rucksacks and set off down the cliff again.

Determined to manage the descent unaided rather than subject herself to the barrage of emotions that came with Jed's touch, Amber set off ahead but she hadn't gone far when she stumbled. Panic seized her as she felt herself fall then Jed grabbed her and steadied her.

'Let's forget about pride and independence and get you down in one piece.' He slipped his arm around her waist.

She nodded numbly, using every ounce of willpower she possessed to stop herself leaning back against him as she longed to do, and they set off down the cliff together.

Jed advised her to put on the travel bands as soon as she got into the little dinghy, to give them chance to work before she went on the *Chenoa*. It was good advice. She hardly felt nauseous at all on the way back so enjoyed the journey. The sea was lovely and calm, the scenery breathtaking, and as she leaned over the rail with the gentle breeze blowing her hair, she thought that she'd never felt happier.

'How are you feeling? Have you got your sea legs yet?' Jed asked her, leaning against the rail besides her.

She turned towards him, smiling, 'I'm fine,' she said. 'These travel bands are marvellous.'

'So you'll be OK to go sailing with Randy tomorrow then?'

She didn't want to think about that. The thought of playing a part, trying to fit in, pretending to be something she wasn't so that Randy would be interested in her felt so wrong. She'd felt so natural and free with Jed. He accepted her for who she was and was such easy company. *If only Jed was a millionaire,* she thought, *then all my problems would be solved.* She could marry him instead

What was she thinking? Of course she couldn't! She could never marry Jed for money. It wouldn't be right. She cared too much for him.

'Amber?'

Jed's voice snapped her out of her thoughts and made her realise she hadn't answered him yet. What was it he had asked her?

'I asked if you'd be OK to go sailing with Randy tomorrow?' he repeated, looking at her curiously.

'Oh yes, I'll be fine,' she said brightly. Too brightly. 'Thanks to you. It was kind of you to bring me on this practice trip.'

'No problem,' he replied. 'It's been good to have the company – and the help. I don't think I could have managed those pups all by myself.'

'So what are your plans now?' she asked him. 'When do you need to get the yacht back to America?'

'There's no immediate rush,' Jed replied. 'I'll set sail the weekend, I think.'

This weekend she would be going back home too. She would never see Jed again. A wave of desolation swept over her as she realised how much she would miss him.

'That's when I'm going home too,' she said.

'I know.' He was staring out at the ocean, his face expressionless.

She longed to ask him if she would he miss her as she would him

Don't be stupid, Amber. You've only known each other a couple of days.

A couple of days that had left an indelible impression on her. Jed would be hard to forget, she acknowledged. He'd stirred feelings in her she didn't know she possessed.

For a while, they stood against the rail, side by side, gazing out at the sea, both lost in their thoughts. Then Coombe Bay Marina came into sight and Jed went to the cockpit to steer the boat in.

Amber felt a flutter of trepidation as they approached the marina. Now it was back to reality. Back to her Millionaire Plan. Back to life without Jed, because for her own peace of mind she had to cut him out of her life. Right now. Today. Because if she got any closer to him, allowed herself to explore her feelings for him, there was no way she would be able to marry Randy.

Chapter Seven

Rule number 7: Cultivate the art of flirting and body language.

Amber had sent Randy a text, as promised, to say she was on her way home. He must have sat in the café waiting for them to return, because as they approached the marina, she'd spotted him sitting at one of the tables, drinking a cup of coffee. He waved, finished his drink, and came over to meet her.

'Hello, darling!' Randy kissed her on the cheek as soon as she stepped off the boat and linked his arm through hers. 'I've booked a table for lunch in a lovely restaurant.'

'I need to change first,' she told him. 'I'm not exactly dressed for a restaurant.'

'Sure, babe. I'll drop you home and wait for you.' He propelled her by the elbow away from the yacht.

Amber turned to say goodbye to Jed but he'd disappeared. *He went below deck pretty quick*, she thought. Probably glad to get rid of her. He'd been very quiet all morning and she guessed that he regretted last night as much as she did and was only too pleased that Tess had disturbed them before things had gone even further.

'You're a bit quiet. How was it on the island?' Randy asked, as he pressed the remote to open the doors of his sleek Ferrari. 'You and Curtess get on OK?'

'Sure. Not that we saw that much of each other,' she said quickly. 'Jed was busy taking photographs and I had my hands full looking after Tess and the pups. Nothing went on between us.' She added just in case he was wondering.

'I didn't think it would. Why should you bother with a no-hoper like Curtess when you've got me?' He opened the car door and got in, leaving her to walk to the passenger side and open the door herself. Not that it bothered her. Her generation didn't expect to have doors opened for them. Women today were independent. They didn't need a man to look after them.

Yeah, right, Amber. That's why you're trying to hook yourself a millionaire.

She sank into the luxurious leather seat and closed the door. Randy started the engine, put the car into gear, checked his mirrors and drove off. *He's not jealous at all,* she realised. And why should he be? As he said, someone like Jed couldn't compete with him.

Like hell, he couldn't. Jed was way out of Randy's league in looks, sheer magnetism, and personality.

But he wasn't a millionaire. And that's why Randy was so confident. He knew that Amber wouldn't turn down the chance of snaring him for a fling with a nobody like Jed. His cock-sure confidence made her angry and she longed to show him that he was wrong. Money didn't matter to her. She judged a man by what he was not what he had.

Except she didn't, did she?

The old Amber did but the new Amber was only interested in a man for his money.

She had nothing to be ashamed of. She wasn't after the money for herself. Besides, men like Randy knew some women only married them for their money. They only married themselves if it was financially advantageous. Like to gain an inheritance, as in Randy's case. She and Randy would both be doing each other a favour.

'It was nice of you to postpone the sailing trip until tomorrow so I can come with you,' she told Randy.

'That's OK, a couple of the others couldn't make today either,' he replied, airily.

So he hadn't postponed it just for her. Why should he? She wasn't that important to him.

Callie and Simon were in the flat when Amber and Randy walked in. Callie pointedly eyed the outfit Amber was wearing but didn't say anything. *I guess I'll get the third degree later,* Amber thought as she went to change. She'd agreed to meet Randy for dinner that evening so he could introduce her to a couple of the others who were going sailing the next day.

Callie was out when she got home, but Amber noticed she had a missed call from her mother. Probably to tell her how the house sale was progressing. She'd better return the call and find out how things were.

'Hello.' Her mother's voice sounded wobbly, as if she'd been crying.

'Mum! Are you OK?' Amber asked anxiously. 'Is Dad alright?'

'Oh, Amber, I'm fine, dear. Just a bit shook up.'

'Why? What's happened?'

'I don't want to worry you, dear.'

'Mum, if you don't tell me, I'll cancel my holiday and come home.'

She heard her mother take a deep breath. 'Well ... oh, it's so awful. I can hardly bring myself to tell you.' She was gabbling so much Amber could barely understand what she was saying.

'Mum, what's happened? What is it?' she asked.

'Oh, darling. We had the bailiff here this morning.' Her mother's voice faltered. 'Can you imagine it? We weren't even dressed. He banged on the door so loud your dad almost had another heart attack.'

'A bailiff!' Things must be worse than she'd realised. 'Why, Mum? Do you owe some money to someone?'

'We haven't been able to pay the Council Tax bill. Your father didn't tell me.' He mother stifled a sob. 'He said he didn't want to worry me.'

Amber could just imagine how her parents had felt. They'd always paid their bills on time, prided themselves on never owing a penny. 'Did they take anything, Mum?' she asked, anxiously.

'No, not yet. They've given us another month but they priced up the car. It was awful. Dreadful. I'm sure all the neighbours were watching. This ... man ... stood there with his notebook and pen and walked all around the car, writing notes on his clipboard how much it was worth. Everyone could see what he was doing.' She gulped. 'If we don't pay the bill they're going to seize the car and sell it. Your father was so shook up he had to go and lie down. They can't really take our car, can they, Amber? What will we do without a car?'

How could she tell her that the bailiff could take the car and any other of their possessions? Amber found out how much the bill was and promised – despite her mother's protestations – to put the money in her parent's bank account right away. It would mean being overdrawn, but she was due to be paid in a couple of days.

Well, that settles it, Amber thought when she'd finally managed to calm her mother down and end the phone call. She had to get the money to help her parents out before the stress killed one of them. She had no choice but to go sailing with Randy and hope he liked her enough to want to get involved with her. She dialled her bank, transferred the money to her parent's bank account, then went for a shower before going to bed.

Callie was waiting for her when she got up the next morning. Wrapped in her fluffy pink bathrobe, painting her nails burgundy.

'OK, spill,' she said, looking us Amber walked in. 'I want to know everything that went on between you and Jed on Blyte Island. And I mean everything.

In your dreams! 'Like I said, we had to stop over to

look after the warden's dog. She had the pups later that night. When the relief warden arrived today we came home.'

'And that was it?' Callie narrowed her eyes as she scrutinised Amber's face. 'No flirting, no kissing?

Amber felt her cheeks burn and quickly bent her head, busying herself taking off her shoes but Callie had obviously already spotted her guilty flush.

'I knew it!' She groaned. 'Please tell me that you didn't sleep with him.'

'Of course I didn't! What do you take me for?' Amber retorted. 'We just … er … kissed, that's all. In the heat of the moment.'

'That's it? One kiss?' Callie demanded.

Well, two kisses, actually but there's no way she was admitting it. 'Yes. Now can we leave the inquisition until another day? I've got to go out in a minute. I'm going sailing with Randy, remember.'

'Hang on, not like that you can't!' Callie got to her feet. 'Remember rule number five: Never let him see you looking anything but your best.'

Amber glanced down at her navy shorts and white T-shirt. 'What's wrong with these? I'm going sailing, not out for dinner,' she pointed out.

'The shorts are too dowdy and the T-shirt is too plain. Hang on.' Callie hurried into her bedroom and came out again holding a short white sundress. 'Wear this, white suits you and is more feminine than shorts.'

Amber sighed but took it in her bedroom to change. After all, Callie had never had a shortage of boyfriends, so maybe she should listen to her.

'That's better.' Callie nodded when Amber came back out.

'Good, now I've got to go! I'm late.' She hurried out before Callie could decide that she needed to change her shoes or do something with her hair.

'Remember it's Randy you want to snare, not Jed!' Callie shouted as Amber pulled the door shut.

She had no trouble spotting the *Daisy Star*. It was a small sailing yacht right at the front of the marina, just as Randy had said. He must have been looking out for her because he leant over the rails, shouting and waving as soon as he saw her.

'Amber! Come on board, we're having some champagne before we set off!'

Champagne this time of the morning, Amber thought as she went aboard the yacht. Randy and Jed were so totally different to each other.

She politely refused the glass of champagne Randy offered her, settling for a glass of freshly squeezed orange juice instead, and smiled brightly as they joined other guests, who were tucking into strawberries and cream with their champagne.

'Didn't I see you at the party on Lord Guy's yacht?' a woman Randy introduced as Tamara asked.

Amber had recognised her instantly, it was the blonde in the tight red dress who'd been all over Jed. She flushed, hoping Tamara hadn't noticed how drunk Amber had been. 'Yes, that's right. I went with some friends. It was a good night, wasn't it?' she replied pleasantly.

'It certainly was.' Tamara raised a thinly-pencilled eyebrow questioningly. 'Hasn't your boyfriend come with you?'

'Boyfriend?' *She means Jed*. Of course, she must have seen them arrive – or even leave – together.

'Jed's not my boyfriend. He's ... just a friend.'

'Oh, I see.' Tamara picked up a strawberry, dipped it into a dish of cream, and bit the top off. 'Well, if you're not with him you won't mind if I make a play for him, will you?'

That stunned her for a moment. 'Er, no, of course not,'

she replied. 'Feel free.'

'Great.' Tamara dipped the rest of the strawberry into the cream, popped it into her mouth, and walked off, leaving Amber staring after her and wondering just why the thought of Tamara and Jed together disturbed her.

'Are you enjoying yourself?' Randy sat down beside her.

She nodded. 'It's a lovely yacht. Is it yours?'

'Yes, a birthday present from my father. I've had it a couple of years now.'

Imagine being that rich! Amber thought of the Christmas presents she'd had off her parents; handbags, perfume, a DVD player – all very much appreciated but not in the same league as a yacht.

'Which just shows you how spoilt our Randy is,' Tamara had returned, with a glass of champagne. She sat down beside Randy. 'Daddy's little rich boy, aren't you, darling?' she teased, stroking his hair.

Randy grinned. 'If my father wants to spoil me, who am I to stop him?'

'What do you do?' Amber asked curiously. 'Work, I mean.'

'Work? Randy!' Tamara almost shrieked with laughter. 'I don't think Randy's ever worked a day in his life.'

'Of course I have. I work extremely hard...at enjoying myself.' Randy jested.

Amber couldn't help thinking how different their worlds were. Randy's life seemed one long party with no real purpose to it. And his friends seemed the same. Whereas everyone she knew spent most of their time working. Look at her father, he had never had a day off sick until his heart attack.

The others joined them and were soon chatting away; talking about the exotic countries they went to for holidays, the night clubs, the clothes. Amber smiled a lot and joined in with the odd comments, but felt a little too out of her depth to say much. Randy sat beside her, gently stroking her arm now and again as he entertained them all with his witty anecdotes about some of the people he'd met. He was so funny – although sometimes a bit cruel – she couldn't help laughing.

They sailed for a couple of hours and Amber was relieved she didn't feel nauseous once thanks to Jed's travel bands. *It had been a lovely afternoon*, she thought happily, as she stood at the rails, looking out to sea. Just as she'd done yesterday when she went sailing with Jed. The two sailing trips had been so different. As Jed and Randy were. Yet both enjoyable in their own way.

'Have you had fun?' Randy asked, putting his arm lightly around her shoulder as the marina came into sight.

'Yes, I have. Thank you.' She smiled at him. 'I meant to ask you, are you taking part in the race? It's on Friday, isn't it?'

'No, I've come down just to watch. Do you fancy keeping me company? We can watch on board the yacht?'

'I'd love to. Thank you.'

'Great. Now how about dinner before the party tonight? I know a lovely little waterfront restaurant, ideal for an intimate meal.'

Intimate. She wasn't sure she liked the idea of that but nodded. 'Sounds good.'

So, at seven fifteen, Amber, clad in the backless red dress Callie had insisted she wore, sat by the dressing table putting the finishing touches to her make up while Callie sat cross-legged on the bed behind her, reading out vitally important points from the 'How to Hook a Millionaire' book.

'Wear the dark red lipstick. It's sexier,' she said as Amber picked up a pearly pink one. 'Men like Randy want to seen with women that other men lust over. It makes them feel good.'

Amber sighed and picked up the dark red lipstick. She was getting a bit sick of hearing what men like Randy wanted.

'And remember, rule number seven, "Cultivate the art or flirting and body language.' Let him know you're interested in him but don't be too eager. And don't sleep with him tonight, even if he begs you".'

'As if I would,' Amber retorted, looking aghast.

'Well, he'll expect you to soon,' Callie told her. 'But hold out a bit. Men like Randy are used to women falling over themselves to get into bed with them so if you keep him waiting a while he'll look on you as a challenge.'

Amber had every intention of keeping Randy waiting – right up to the wedding night, she thought, blotting her lips with a tissue. Now if it was Jed ...

Here she went again. She had to get him out of her mind. She was going out with Randy now, for goodness sake.

Dinner was very pleasant. Randy was entertaining, if a bit loud – a few times his raucous laugh made the other diners turn around to stare at them – he was good company, good looking. *I think I could make this work*, Amber thought, as Randy helped her on with the ivory fur shrug Callie had loaned her.

She felt a bit nervous walking into the ballroom but Callie and Simon were already there and waved for them to join them.

'You look stunning,' Callie said. Then she leaned over and whispered in Amber's ear. 'Randy can't take his eyes off you. I knew that dress was a good choice for you.'

Amber glanced around the room, telling herself she wasn't looking for Jed. But she was. Then she spotted him, deep in conversation with Tamara, who was giggling and hanging onto his every word. As if sensing her eyes upon him, Jed glanced over his shoulder. He smiled. Tamara followed his gaze and raised her glass triumphantly.

Well, she didn't waste much time, did she, Amber thought, stifling the surge of jealousy which ran through her. It seemed like Tamara and Jed would soon be an item. Well, so what if they were? She had to get over this silly infatuation she had for Jed and concentrate on Randy.

Randy was attentive to her all evening, rarely leaving her side and only dancing a couple of dances with anyone else. He was flirtatious and fun and Amber responded in the same manner. To her surprise she enjoyed herself immensely.

'I'll go and get us some more champagne,' he said, kissing her on the cheek.

'Just orange juice for me, please,' she told him, wanting to keep a clear head.

He winked. 'Shame, you're far more interesting when you've been drinking champagne.'

If only you knew how interesting, she thought as she watched him weave his way through the crowd to the bar. She felt herself flush as she recalled waking up in bed on Jed's yacht. There was no way she was going to let anything like that happen again.

Instinctively, she looked around for Jed and saw him whirling around the dance floor with Tamara, their arms wrapped around each other, their heads thrown back as they laughed.

She turned away and smiled at Randy as he put the glasses down on the table. 'Shall we dance?'

'Sure.' He nodded, holding out his arms.

She sensed Tamara was watching her so forced herself to concentrate on her steps, following Randy's lead and trying her best to keep time to the music. To her relief she got the hang of it and was soon gliding almost effortlessly around the dance floor.

As she passed Tamara and Jed, he nodded approvingly

and winked at her. Tamara immediately buried her head into Jed's shoulder as if driving home the fact that he was with her.

You can have him, Amber thought as Randy kissed her on the forehead. *He's all yours.*

'Can we go somewhere quiet and talk?' Randy asked when the dance was finished. 'How about a walk along the marina front?'

She nodded and picked up her shrug. 'I wouldn't mind a bit of fresh air,' she admitted.

Her mind was racing as they walked out into the cool, night air. Randy had been good company all evening, and from the way he had held her when they danced, the tender way he'd treated her, she was sure he was going to ask her to go out with him. To officially be his girlfriend. And if he did, she was going to accept. When she went home the weekend they could still continue dating, then perhaps things would get more serious between them.

Randy put his arm around her shoulders as they walked along. 'I'm going to put my cards on the table, Amber, and make you a proposition,' he said solemnly. He squeezed her shoulder. 'I like you Amber. I like you a lot. And I think you like me.'

'Yes, I do. Well, I mean I hardly know you ...' What was she doing? This is where she was supposed to pretend she was instantly attracted to him. *Remember rule number seven: cultivate the art of flirting and body language.* 'We get on well,' she added quickly, 'and I've enjoyed the time we've spent together.'

'So have I.' He pulled her down onto a nearby bench, held her hand, and sat facing her. 'The thing is, I think we can both help each other out.' His hold on her hand tightened. 'I need your help to claim my inheritance. My father tied most of it up, you see, stipulating that I had to wait until I was thirty to claim it – and I get extra, quite a lot extra, if I'm married with a baby on the way by then.

So what do you think? Will you marry me? You'll have a life of luxury in return.'

This is what she wanted, had planned for, but now it was in her reach her nerve failed her. Could she go ahead and marry Randy, someone she had just met and didn't love? Could she be his wife, with everything that went with it?

'You don't have to answer now, think about it and let me know tomorrow,' Randy said. 'I know it's a big thing to ask of you but I believe we can make it work. You can still live your life and I can live mine. All I ask of you is to be discreet.'

'You mean ...?' Amber stared at him, stunned.

'It'll be purely a business arrangement. We'll have to have a baby, of course, and I'll make sure you never want for anything. But I won't ask anything else from you.'

A business arrangement. So she wouldn't be misleading him, it would all be above board. It sounded ideal so why was she hesitating?

Because it sounds too cold and calculating. That's why, she told herself. She'd always planned on getting married for love. Of being wooed. Proposed to properly, being swept off her feet with the emotion of it all.

'Thank you. I'll think it over and let you know my decision tomorrow,' she managed to stammer, her head reeling. What should she do?

Amber got up early the next morning and had a stroll along the marina front to clear her head. And somehow found herself heading towards Jed's yacht.

He was on deck, obviously preparing to go for a sail, dressed in just a pair of denim shorts. For a moment she stood watching him, admiring the easy expertise in his handling of the yacht, the way his hair curled at the nape of his neck, his lean suntanned torso ...

OK, that's enough drooling.

She waved. 'Morning! Did you enjoy the party last night?'

'Not as much as you seemed to,' he replied. 'I don't think you needed those sailing lessons after all.'

'Perhaps not.' She hesitated as she watched Jed check the sails. 'Are you off for another sail?'

'Sort of.'

He turned to face her and something about the expression on his face made her catch her breath.

'Where are you going?'

'Home.'

'Home?'

'Back to America.'

America? That meant she would never see him again. Stunned, she just stared at him.

'You seem a bit surprised. I told you my boss flew home last week and I had to sail the yacht back myself,' Jed reminded her.

'Yes, but you didn't say you were going so soon. I thought you were staying until the weekend.' *Steady on, Amber, don't let him see how upset you are.*

Just why was she so upset anyway?

'What difference does it make?' His eyes narrowed as he looked at her. 'I was going home the weekend anyway. What does it matter to you if I leave a few days earlier?

It shouldn't matter. But it did. It mattered a lot. She didn't stop to examine why she just clutched at straws to keep him here. 'You promised to teach me how to mix with Randy's set,' she stammered.

'I don't think you need me to do that. From what I hear, Randy seems to have decided you're the one to help him get his inheritance.' His eyes met hers. 'I presume you've accepted his proposal.'

'You know! Who told you?'

'Randy did. He couldn't wait to brag about it. He's confident you'll say yes. And you will, of course, won't you? It's what you've been planning all along.'

'You make it sound so ... heartless.'

He raised an eyebrow questioningly. 'Sorry. I must have got it wrong. Do I take it that you love each other?'

'No,' she had to admit.

'Then I think heartless is a good way to describe your relationship, don't you?'

'I guess so.' She tried to keep her voice steady so he wouldn't guess how distraught she felt at the thought of him leaving. Going out of her life forever. 'When are you going?'

'In about half an hour.'

If she'd arrived any later he'd have gone and she'd never have had the chance to say goodbye.

She didn't want to say goodbye. She wanted to beg him to stay.

Don't be stupid. It's better if he goes. Then you can just concentrate on marrying Randy.

'Goodbye then,' she said, holding out her hand, hoping he wouldn't notice that it was shaking. 'Have a safe journey home and thanks for your help.'

He took her hand and shook it briefly, his face an impenetrable mask, his eyes cold and distant. 'Bye, Amber. Take care. Don't let the rich set change you.'

He didn't care that he wouldn't see her again. She meant nothing to him. A sob catching at her throat, she pulled her hand away before he could see the tears in her eyes and turned to go. He reached out, grabbed her shoulder, and spun her round to face him again.

'I think we can do better than a handshake.' His mouth was on hers and she was lost in the ecstasy of his kisses. Again.

Pull away before you get in too deep, the sensible voice in her head warned her. She knew she should but she couldn't. She wanted to stay like this forever, just be with Jed, forget all about Randy and the Millionaire Plan.

Randy! Oh no, she was supposed to be meeting him for lunch at twelve to give him her answer.

'Don't tell me you're going to meet Randy?' There was an edge to his voice.

She bit her lip. 'I've got to ...'

'Dammit, Amber!' He released her. 'I can't believe you're going straight from my arms to meet another man.'

'And you're going back home – to America!' she retorted sharply, tears welling up in her eyes as reality set in. So they were attracted to each other. Had shared a few kisses, it changed nothing. At least not to Jed.

She had to get away.

Jed grabbed her arm, stopped her. 'Forget about Randy. Marry me.'

'Marry you?' she repeated, staring at him in confusion. 'Why?'

'Because I love you,' he said simply. 'And I think that you love me too. Don't you?'

He loved her.

Amber felt like she was bursting with happiness. He loved her. And she loved him too. She realised that now. The wonder of it brought tears to her eyes and she nodded, unable to speak.

He cupped her chin with his hands. 'Say it. Tell me you love me.'

'I love you,' she said softly, her eyes meeting his and seeing the love she felt reflected back in his gaze.

He released his breath and pulled her into his arms. 'I knew you did.'

For a moment she was swamped with overwhelming happiness. Then reality kicked in.

'I love you,' she repeated. 'But I can't marry you.'

'What?'

Her heart felt like it was breaking as she pulled away from him and stared down at her hands, twisting them nervously. 'I've told you. I've got to marry someone with money so I can help my parents. It's my fault they're in this mess. Please try and understand.' Her eyes pleaded with him.

'How the hell am I supposed to understand that you love me but intend to marry someone else?' he demanded.

'I don't *want* to marry anyone else, Jed. I want to marry you,' she told him, tears streaming down her face. 'But I can't. I just can't.'

'So you're prepared to let me walk out of your life. To go back to America and never see you again?'

A sob wrenched from her throat. 'Can't you see I have no choice?'

'You do have a choice, Amber. There's always a choice.'

'But my parents …'

He swore. 'There must be another way your parents can sort out the mess they're in. You can't sacrifice your life for them.'

Roughly, he pulled her to him and kissed her, passionately, desperately. She clung to him, returning his kisses with fervour.

'I love you,' the words came from deep within him.

'I love you too,' she covered his face with kisses. 'I want to marry you. Really, I do.'

'Then say yes. Marry me.'

She longed to say yes. Her heart belonged to Jed, how could she marry someone else?

She had to get away, think things through. She traced his lips with her finger. 'I need a bit of time to think. Get my head straight. It's been such a shock.'

He gazed at her, his expression unfathomable. What should she do?

'Jed?' Her voice quivered. 'Can I think about it?'

'OK, I'll give you until tomorrow morning,' he agreed, releasing her. 'If you decide you don't want to marry me then I'll sail back to America.'

'Thank you.' Her voice was a mere whisper.

Jed stepped back, as if putting distance between them. 'Remember, if I don't hear from you by noon tomorrow, I'm sailing home.'

It hurt him that she hadn't instantly accepted his proposal but he knew it must have been a shock to her. It was a shock to him too. He couldn't believe he'd proposed to her but it was what he wanted. He loved her and she loved him, he knew that. If only she wasn't torn between this blind loyalty to her parents. She probably had to come to terms with the fact that if she married him she couldn't bail them out and they would lose their home.

Only they wouldn't, would they? If Amber married him she would have more money than she could spend in a lifetime. But she didn't know that yet, and he didn't want her to. He wanted her to believe that he was just a normal, working guy when she accepted his offer of marriage. Not until they were married would he tell her the truth. That he owned this yacht and a large property company in America. That he was not in fact a millionaire, but a billionaire.

Chapter Eight

Rule number 8: Don't wear your heart on your sleeve, keep him guessing.

When did I fall in love with Jed, Amber wondered as she strolled along the beach, deep in thought. Was it the first time she'd seen him? She wasn't sure, she hadn't even acknowledged that it was love she felt for him until today. And when had he fallen for her? Perhaps he didn't realise until today either. Until he thought he'd lost her to Randy.

Just thinking about him gave her a warm glow in her heart. How could she marry Randy when her heart belonged to Jed? How could she let him go back to America and never see him again?

She'd sent a text to Randy, telling him she was still thinking about his proposal and needed a bit more time. She promised to meet him later that night. Then she switched off her phone. She didn't want him to phone or text her, try to persuade her. She needed to think and get her head straight.

She stopped to pick up a stone and throw it into the sea, skimming the surface of the water. What should she do? How could she put her happiness before her parents' welfare? She was sure that being forced to sell their home would cause her father to have another, possibly fatal, heart attack. Could she risk it happening?

But she loved Jed so much and was sure he loved her, too. She didn't want to lose him. If she rejected him she would regret it for the rest of her life.

She remembered her dad always telling her that there

was more than one way to solve a problem. Perhaps there was another way she could help them out rather than marry a millionaire. She'd never been happy with the idea. It was a wild scheme of Callie's that she'd allowed herself to get carried away with. She didn't want loads of money for herself, she just wanted to save her parents' home.

Then it hit her. She could sell her flat. There would still be a considerable sum left over once she'd paid off her mortgage. She could give it to her parents so they could pay off their debts and stay in their beloved home. She wouldn't need the flat if she married Jed, would she? She'd be living with him, wherever that was. It suddenly occurred to her that she hadn't asked Jed where they would be living but she guessed he would want her to come to America with him. Maybe she could get a job, persuade him to give up working for his millionaire boss and concentrate on photography instead. It was the ideal solution. She didn't know why she hadn't thought of it before.

She hugged her arms around her, wanting to shout, to let everyone know that she was free. Free to marry Jed.

What if he'd changed his mind? After all, a few hours had passed since she left him. He said he'd wait until tomorrow for her answer but what if he thought she couldn't love him enough to marry him if she had to think about it? She reached for her phone to ring him, then hesitated. Should she tell him in person? But what if he was about to set sail and she missed him? She had to phone him.

He answered on the second ring.

'Amber?' His voice sounded cautious.

'Yes, Jed, Yes. I will marry you,' she said. 'That is, if you still want me to?'

'Oh, sweetheart. Of course I still want you to! It's what I want more than anything in the world.'

'Me too.'

'Where are you?'

'On the beach, by the pier.'

'Stay there, I'll come and get you.'

'No, I'll come to you. I want to,' she insisted.

'I'll be waiting,' he whispered.

He ran down to meet her as she approached the marina, swooping her up in his arms, to the amusement of some passers-by.

'Did you mean it?' he asked. 'You're really going to marry me?'

'Yes!' she shouted. 'Yes, yes!'

Then they were kissing each other and, arms entwined around each other's waist, climbing onto the deck of the yacht, still hugging and kissing, too caught up in their happiness to care what anyone else thought.

'What about Randy?' Jed asked.

'I'm going to meet him later and tell him. I'm sure he'll find someone else to marry.' She shrugged. After all, it's not as if we're even an item.'

'So nothing happened between you?'

'Nothing at all,' she said solemnly. 'I was never attracted to Randy in that way. Besides,' she added mischievously, 'Rule number six forbids it.'

'And what does rule number six say?' Jed asked, nibbling her ear.

'Don't get intimate with him too quickly. Keep him waiting,' she replied. 'Good job you're not a millionaire, isn't it? I'd have trouble keeping that rule with you.'

Little do you know that you've got yourself a millionaire by breaking nearly every rule in the book. Jed enfolded her in his arms and tried to imagine the look on her face when, on their wedding day, he confessed who he really was. The fact that she'd chosen him above Randy, without knowing his true identity, meant a lot to him. He'd spent years fending off the attentions of gold-diggers, then

Melissa had almost ensnared him. He needed to know that Amber was marrying him because she loved him, not for his money.

'What about your parents?' he asked.

'I've thought of a way to sort that out,' she told him, threading her fingers through his hair, pulling his head towards her. 'Now, are you going to kiss me or not?'

'I certainly am,' he told her. 'In fact, I am going to kiss you so much you'll be dizzy with desire.'

And he did.

'How are you enjoying it in England?' Chloe asked. She'd phoned him for their weekly chat just after Amber had left. 'You're not taking part in the race are you?'

He chuckled. 'No, not my scene. I'm just here to watch.'

'Have you met anyone interesting?'

He knew Chloe meant had he met any women. She'd been trying to match-make him ever since Melissa, saying he couldn't judge half the human race by the behaviour of one woman, but he'd resisted her attempts. He had no intention of getting involved again.

Until he met Amber. And now, after knowing her less than a week he'd proposed to her. Should he tell Chloe? They always talked about things.

'Well?' she asked quickly, as if guessing he was holding something back.

No, he wasn't going to tell her. It sounded too crazy. He'd take Amber over to meet her then Chloe would see how they were meant to be together.

'I met a Lord, even went to a party on his boat,' he told her. He soon had Chloe giggling as he recounted some amusing anecdotes from the party.

'And did you go to that island and take some photos of the birds?' Chloe asked when they'd both finished laughing.

'Yes, I did. I'll email you some of them,' he said. 'It was beautiful island. Mind you, we had a bit of drama there …' He told Chloe all about Mike and having to stay to keep an eye on Tess and the pups, leaving out the bit about Amber going with him. He knew that as soon as he said her name Chloe would know how he felt, and he didn't want to tell her yet.

'Come home, Jed,' Chloe said. 'You've been a hermit long enough. Come back and start living your life again.'

'I will. I'm coming home the end of the week,' he promised. 'Now tell me what my rogues of a nephew and niece have got up to this week.' He was close to Chloe's children, five year old Ryan and two year old Amy, and missed them dearly.

'Believe me, you don't want to know,' Chloe said in mock-exasperation, then proceeded to tell him their latest escapades.

Jed listened to her in amusement. Maybe in a couple of years he and Amber would have children too. He'd never wanted a family before, he'd always been too busy working but now he'd found Amber there was nothing he'd like better.

'Callie! Are you there?' Amber called as she opened the door to the apartment. She couldn't wait to share her news with her friend, knowing that while Callie might tell her she was nuts to choose Jed over Randy, she'd be pleased for her once she knew how much they loved each other.

Silence greeted her.

Obviously, Callie was out. Probably with Simon again. Well, she'd just have to phone her. She took out her mobile phone and called Callie. After a few rings it switched to answerphone. Feeling a bit deflated, Amber left a brief message saying that Jed had proposed and she'd accepted.

Then she fixed herself something to eat and decided to

lie down for a while. She slept for a couple of hours and woke feeling more refreshed. A smile curved her lips as she thought of Jed. She could hardly believe that it was less than a week since they'd met and now they were engaged. Glancing at the clock, she saw that she had an hour before Jed was due to pick her up for dinner. Plenty of time to have a shower and get changed. He'd promised to take her somewhere special to celebrate their engagement.

Callie must still be out, she thought as she turned on the shower, because she knew her friend would have woken her up to try and talk her out of the engagement. Not that there was any chance of her doing that. Jed was the one she wanted. The only one she'd ever want.

Jed got out of the taxi, slipped the driver a fat tip, and looked over at the apartment where Amber was staying, reaching into his jacket pocket to feel the ring box. He'd resisted the urge to buy her the biggest diamond he could find. He didn't want Amber to know the extent of his wealth just yet, but he had wanted to buy her a ring to be proud of, so had selected a delicate diamond set in an unusual twenty-two carat gold clasp. He doubted Amber would know how expensive it was, but if she did guess he'd tell her he got a discount from the jeweller his boss used – one of the perks of the job.

He walked over to the apartment and pressed the buzzer for number 6A.

'Is that you, Jed?' Amber's voice echoed down the intercom.

'Who else are you expecting?' he replied, teasing.

'Come and up.'

With a loud buzz, the doors opened and he stepped through, walked over to the lift and pressed the button for the second floor.

The apartment door was open.

'I'm almost ready,' Amber shouted from the bedroom. 'Pour yourself a drink if you want, there's a bottle of wine in the fridge.'

'No thanks, I'll wait till we have the meal,' Jed replied.

He walked over to the elegant cream sofa – Callie's aunt obviously had good taste – sat down, stretching his legs out in front of him, and leaned back. Something hard dug in his back. Sitting up again, he lifted the cushion and found a magazine stuffed behind it. He recognised the title, it was an upmarket fashion and gossip magazine like the ones Chloe often bought. He idly flicked through the pages and was stunned to see a photo of himself staring back at him. What on earth was he doing in this magazine? He hadn't given any interviews since before his mother died two years ago.

It wasn't an interview, it was a two page spread under the heading 'Single, Solvent, and Sexy'. It featured half a dozen pictures of millionaires, including him and Randy. There was just a small paragraph about him under one photo, with a brief biography of how he'd come to amass his fortune – which they'd grossly understated. Apparently the men were all fodder for any gold-digging female who wanted to hook a millionaire.

Like Amber.

So she knew. She'd been stringing him along, working her ten point plan on him while pretending she was trying to hook Randy.

No, she wasn't that devious.

Then what was the magazine doing stuffed behind the cushion?

Amber had known about him right from the start and set out to ensnare him, telling him how she was worried she couldn't dance, hoping he'd offer to teach her. And when he had, she'd pressed herself close to him, inviting his kiss, returning it with passion. It had all been part of her plan. She'd been playing him and Randy, seeing which one she could get to propose to her first.

But she'd refused his proposal at first.

Just a ploy to make him think she loved him so much she was giving up a millionaire to marry him, hoping to convince him she had no idea he was worth far, far more than Randy. He felt sick to his stomach. He'd been so sure Amber wasn't like all the women who hung about the yachts hoping to hook a millionaire. She'd fooled him with her naïve, innocent act. Pretending she didn't know how to behave in 'rich' society. Getting his sympathy with that story about wanting to help her parents out of a mess. And he'd swallowed it hook, line, and sinker.

No, that wasn't a story, it was true, he was sure it was.

But that didn't change the fact that Amber was only marrying him for his money.

Fool. Idiot. Thinking she had chosen him because she loved him.

He threw the magazine on the table and stood up.

Well, the game was up. He'd found her out just in time.

Single, solvent, and sexy he might be but stupid he wasn't.

There was no way any gold-digger was going to marry him for his money. No way at all.

He strode angrily across the room and out of the apartment.

Chapter Nine

Rule number 9: Once you've hooked him set a date for the wedding right away.

'I'm ready,' Amber said, smiling as she walked out of the bedroom. 'Where are we going or is it a surprise ...'

Her voice tailed off as she realised that Jed wasn't in the room. Where had he gone? He would have had to pass her room to go to the bathroom and the kitchen door was wide open so she could see he wasn't in there. Then she noticed that the front door was slightly open. Perhaps he'd gone to get something out of the car.

Ah, here he is, she thought as she heard footsteps and the rustling of bags outside. No it couldn't be him, the footsteps were too light.

She stared as the door was pushed open and Callie, walked in, her arms laden with bags.

'You're a quick worker,' Callie said, admiration in her voice. She shut the door behind her with her foot. 'It didn't take you long to hook Jed, did it?'

'What? You mean you approve?' Amber asked, surprised. 'I expected you to give me a lecture about how I should marry Randy instead.'

'Of course not. I was chuffed when I got your message. It's obvious that you and Jed have the hots for each other so I was delighted when I read that article. Simon brought it over earlier. He said he thought he recognised Jed from somewhere then he remembered the article. Randy's in it too, you know.'

'Article?' Amber frowned. 'What article?'

'The one in *Scoop* magazine.' Callie deposited the parcels on the sofa, pushing aside the cream scatter cushion first. 'Mind you, I thought I'd hid it well behind that cushion – I wanted to show it you myself so I could see the expression on your face.'

'What magazine? What article? Do you mean one of Jed's wildlife articles?' Amber asked. She'd love to read something he'd written. 'Talking of Jed, did you pass him on the way up? He was waiting for me to get ready but when I came out of the bedroom he'd gone.'

'He's just gone off in a taxi. I thought he was going home.'

'Gone off in a taxi?' Amber repeated, bewildered. 'But we were supposed to be going out to dinner to celebrate our engagement. I don't understand ... what are you staring at?'

Callie, a stricken look on her face, was staring down at carpet.

Amber followed her gaze and saw a magazine, open, face-down on the floor besides the coffee table. As if someone had read something they didn't like and had thrown it down in disgust.

'Did Jed sit on the sofa?' Callie's voice sounded strangled, as if she had to force it out.

'I'm not sure. I guess so.' Amber stared at the magazine, a dozen questions flitting through her mind. Had Jed read his article and been annoyed by something in it? She'd heard how editors hacked articles, omitting some things and adding others. Is that why he'd taken off without a word? Because he was angry? But why not tell her? Was he coming back? What about the table they'd booked?

Callie bent down to pick up the magazine, then handed it, still open to Amber.

'You'd better read this,' she said.

Amber took it off her and glanced down. Frowning, she

saw the heading 'Single, Solvent, and Sexy' above some pictures of dishy men. What had this to do with Jed? Then she spotted his face smiling out at her from the middle of the page and her knees went weak. Her eyes fixed on the article, her hands shaking, she sat down on the sofa and read the paragraph underneath Jed's photo. It was short but long enough to tell her that far from being a hired hand Jed was a millionaire – no, make that billionaire. Apparently he owned a string of property in America. A property mogul, the article called him. She shook her head in disbelief. It couldn't be true.

Couldn't it? Remember the casual way he fitted into the 'rich society', the air of confidence he exuded. That luxury yacht was his, so were the designer clothes. He was loaded.

Why had he pretended that he worked for a millionaire instead of telling her the truth?

It took her all of five seconds to work out the answer.

Because he didn't want her to marry him for his money. And now that's exactly what he thought she was doing. He must have found the magazine when she was getting changed, read the article, and jumped to the conclusion she'd hid it behind the cushion.

No wonder he'd walked out.

'You haven't read it, have you?' Callie asked.

Amber shook her head. 'Jed must have moved the cushion and found it. I guess he thought I left it there. That I only agreed to marry him because I'd found out he was rich.'

'That's rubbish. Everyone can see that you two are mad about each other.'

'Is it?' she demanded. 'And why exactly did you bring that article to show me? Wasn't it to persuade me to try and hook Jed instead of Randy? Before you found out how rich he was you kept warning me to stay away from him, not to get involved.'

'That's because you wanted to marry a millionaire to help your parents out.'

'Jed knows it too. That's why he's walked out on me.'

'Surely if you tell him that you didn't know he was rich when you agreed to marry him everything will be OK again.' Callie sat down beside her. 'I'll explain that it was me who brought the magazine home this morning. And that you were already out so never had chance to read it.'

'Don't you see that even if Jed does believe you I still couldn't marry him?' Amber blinked back the tears. 'Jed didn't tell me who he was because he didn't trust me. I told him myself that I'd come here to try and hook a millionaire.'

'You fell in love with Jed despite that. You agreed to marry him when you thought he was poor,' Callie pointed out.

'Even if I manage to persuade him of that, the doubt will always be there in the back of his mind. He didn't trust me enough to tell me the truth, Callie.' Amber's voice broke into a sob. 'So there's no way I could marry him even if he believed me and still wanted to marry me.'

She ran into the bedroom, slamming the door behind her. Sobbing uncontrollably, she flung herself on the bed, letting the salty tears spill down her cheeks. Her heart had been smashed into smithereens and she'd never be able to put it back together again.

Sometime later, when the worst of the tears had subsided, Callie knocked on the door. 'Amber, can I come in?'

Amber wiped her arm across her eyes and sat up. 'Yes,' she sniffed.

The door opened and her friend walked in, carrying two mugs and a box of tissues. 'I've brought you emergency supplies.' She sat down on the edge of bed, held out the box of tissues, and waited patiently while Amber took one, wiped her eyes, and blew her nose, then held out one of the mugs.

'Thanks.' Amber took the mug and her eyes filled with tears again when she noticed the pink marshmallow floating on the top of the hot chocolate. Jed had made her hot chocolate with a marshmallows when they'd been on Blyte Island. The day she'd first realised how strong her feelings were for him.

And now she'd lost him.

Swivelling the mug around so she could grip the handle, she took a sip. It was hot and sweet.

'I put in two sugars. I thought you needed it.' Callie looked at her friend's swollen eyes and tear-stained face. 'You really love Jed, don't you?'

Amber sniffed. 'Yes, I do.'

'He loves you too. I know he does.'

'Maybe he does but it doesn't make any difference. We're finished.'

Finished before they'd even really begun.

'If you explained ...'

'It would make no difference. Don't you see that? I told you, he doesn't trust me. And without trust a relationship is dead.'

Just like their love. Only it wasn't dead for her, was it? She felt that she would always carry the loss and pain with her. Tears spilled from her eyes and rolled down her cheeks.

Callie reached out and took the mug from her, placing it on the floor besides the bed. 'I'm sorry, Amber. It's all my fault,' she said miserably. 'If I'd have taken that magazine into my room instead of shoving it behind the cushion none of this would have happened. You'd still be engaged to Jed. I've ruined everything.'

'It's not your fault,' Amber told her. 'I don't blame you. Once I'd read that article I wouldn't have been able to marry Jed anyway. How could I?' She blinked back a tear. 'I'll never be able to marry anyone now. I'll never love anyone like I love Jed.'

'But what about The Millionaire Plan?'

'It's off. It was a stupid idea in the first place. I should never have gone along with it.'

'My fault again,' Callie said quietly. 'I'm the one who talked you into it.'

Her friend looked so contrite that Amber felt guilty for her outburst. After all, Callie had only been trying to help.

She sat back down on the bed. 'We were both trying to help my parents,' she acknowledged. 'But I should have thought about it a bit more. My dad always said there was more than one way to solve a problem.'

'He's right, we'll just have to come up with another money-making plan,' Callie said, eagerly. 'I know that *Ladzmag* are looking for some glamour models and they pay pretty well. I could introduce you to the editor ...' her voice trailed off as she saw the look of outrage on Amber's face. 'I guess you don't fancy it.'

'I most certainly do not!' Amber said. 'And before you come up with even more outrageous ideas I'd better tell you that I've thought of a solution. That's why I agreed to marry Jed. I'm going to sell my flat and give my parents the money to pay off their debts.'

'And where are you going to live?'

Good question. She had intended to live with Jed.

'I guess I'll move back in with my parents until I sort something out.'

'Move back in with your parents?' Now it was Callie's turn to look incredulous. 'I wouldn't fancy that. And what about your job?'

'I could commute, it's not that far.' Amber told her. About an hour's drive, actually, but lots of people commuted to work nowadays.

The catchy tune of Callie's mobile phone ringing in the lounge interrupted them.

'That'll be Simon,' Callie said, standing up. 'I'm

supposed to be going out with him tonight but I could cancel and keep you company …'

Amber shook her head. 'Definitely not. I'd rather be on my own. I've got some thinking to do.'

The rings got louder. Callie hesitated at the door. 'Are you sure?'

'Positive. Now go and answer that before it switches to answerphone.'

There was no word from Jed all evening. Not that Amber expected him to contact her. He knew she'd see the magazine he'd thrown on the floor, guess he'd read the article and realise the engagement was off. There was no need for any contact from either of them. It was obvious they were finished.

She decided to go home the next morning and put her flat on the market. There was nothing to keep her in Coombe Bay anymore. Jed was probably already on his way back to America. She'd phoned Randy, thanked him for his proposal but said she couldn't accept. He'd tried to persuade her but she'd remained adamant. She just wanted to go home and get on with her life.

She had almost finished packing when Callie returned.

'Where are you going?' Callie asked, surprised.

'Home.' Amber snapped the suitcase shut. 'There's no reason for me to stay here anymore so I'd prefer to go home and get my flat on the market. The quicker I sell it the better.'

'Stay until my aunt comes back on Saturday,' Callie coaxed. 'It's only a couple more days. It will do you good to have a bit of a rest. And maybe you and Jed can sort things out.'

Amber shook her head. 'There's no chance of that. I need to get away, Callie. You've got Simon and your friends so you won't be lonely. Besides,' she added, 'I've already booked my seat on the train. I leave at 10.35

tomorrow.'

Callie hugged her. 'I'm going to miss you.'

Amber was shattered but her troubled mind kept her awake. She spent most of the night tossing and turning, trying to block out all thoughts of Jed to no avail. Finally, drifting off as the birds started to sing, she was awake again less than two hours later. Knowing she wouldn't be able to get back to sleep, she decided to get up. It was no good moping around.

She'd showered and was drying her hair when the buzzer rang. For a moment a wild hope leapt in her mind that it might be Jed, that he'd come to talk to her, give her a chance to explain.

'Amber. Are you up?'

Randy. She should have guessed.

'Come on up,' she called down the intercom, pressing the button to open the entrance doors.

She left the front door on the latch and went into the kitchen to put the kettle on, then spooned coffee into the cafeteria. She needed a strong fix of caffeine.

A few minutes later, she heard Randy's footsteps outside.

'The door's open!' she shouted. 'I'm making a coffee. Do you want one?' she asked, poking her head around the kitchen door as Randy walked in.

With his fair hair falling across his eyes and dressed in casual designer slacks and an open-necked shirt, Randy looked every inch a movie star. Which, she guessed, was his intention.

'Black, no sugar,' he said, coming into the kitchen. 'Look, I've been thinking. I proposed much too soon. We need to get to know each other a bit more. Perhaps we could take a ride out today, have lunch at a pub, take in a few sights. What do you think?'

'Sorry, I can't. I'm going home today.'

'Home?' He sounded surprised. 'I thought you and Callie were staying until the weekend.'

The kettle boiled and switched itself off. She poured the hot water into the cafetiere and let it stand for a couple of minutes while she took two mugs out of the cupboard above her head.

'Callie is but I'm not. I'm going home,' she told him.

'Why? Has something come up?'

'You could say that.' She pressed the filter down then poured out the coffee, adding a drop of milk to one mug. She handed the mug of black coffee to Randy. Then perched on one of the bar stools. Randy sat down on the stool besides her.

'Can't you put it off?' he wheedled, putting on his most charming smile.

She shook her head. 'I'm afraid not. I have to go home.'

'What's this? Where are you going?' Callie stumbled into the kitchen, her fluffy bathrobe wrapped around her. 'Oh, hello, Randy.'

'Just in time to help me persuade Amber not to go home,' Randy told her.

'I have been trying to persuade her but she's determined,' Callie replied.

'I'm sorry, Randy, but I've got to go today.' Amber glanced at the clock on the wall. 'In fact, my train leaves in just under an hour.'

'Then at least let me take you to the station,' Randy offered. 'I can get my chauffeur to pick us up.'

It seemed churlish to refuse so she nodded. 'Thank you, I'd appreciate it.'

Jed narrowed his eyes and thrust his hands deep in his pockets as he watched Amber and Randy walk over to his chauffeur-driven Bentley. Randy was carrying a case – obviously Amber's – and they were talking, heads so close they were almost touching.

Well, she didn't waste much time, did she? he thought bitterly.

All night he'd been torturing himself that he'd judged her wrong, telling himself she might not have read the magazine, that Callie or her aunt could have stuffed it behind the cushion and Amber knew nothing about it. Convincing himself that she did love him after all. They had been so good together. Surely it wasn't an act? He wanted to believe in her, in their love.

In the cold light of the morning he'd felt guilty about walking out without giving her a chance to explain so had decided to come back and talk to her, hoping in his heart that he'd misjudged her. Well, he needn't have bothered. He'd been right about her. She was just a gold-digger after his money. Realising her scheme hadn't worked on him, she'd wasted no time in moving on to Randy. After all, there was more than one millionaire to choose from. And by the case she was carrying she'd made her choice and was moving in with him.

He turned away and walked back towards the marina where the *Chenoa* was all ready to sail. It was time for him to go home.

'Don't forget to give me your address,' Randy said as they made their way to the train station.

'What?' she asked, puzzled.

'How can I come and see you if I don't have it? I thought I'd pop over the weekend. We could go to a club or something.'

Oh dear, he thought she still wanted to go on seeing him. She'd better put him straight.

'Actually, I'm going to be so busy I don't think I'll have much time to socialise.'

'You'll have some time off, surely?'

When they reached the train station he insisted on

coming to the platform to see her off. 'You're not going to disappear out of my life, are you? I thought we were an item now.' He sounded disappointed. Hurt.

So he really was interested in her. She felt a bit guilty but reminded herself that a man like Randy would soon find someone else to replace her.

'We've had some fun but I'm going home now, back to my normal life,' she said.

'That doesn't mean the fun has to stop. You haven't got a boyfriend at home, have you?' he asked.

'No, of course not. It's just that, well, we move in different circles, Randy.'

'We don't have too. You could marry me and move in the same circles.'

She met his gaze. 'I told you, I can't marry you. But thank you for asking me.'

'Why not? We're good together. Marrying would be a good financial move for both of us.'

No talk of love. But then she didn't expect him too. Neither of them loved each other.

'So you can get your inheritance?'

'And you can live in luxury,' he reminded her.

It was what she'd wanted, planned for. But not anymore. She didn't want to marry anyone but Jed. And that was impossible.

She let Randy down as gently as she could, telling him she wasn't ready for a relationship and could never marry just for money. He sulked and pleaded, trying to cajole her address out of her so they could at least keep in touch but she was adamant.

'If you change your mind, let me know,' he said, holding tight.

He actually seemed quite upset and she felt bad for letting him believe she was interested in him.

Thankfully, her train arrived and Randy realised his hold. She picked up her case. 'I'm sorry, but it's been lovely knowing you,' she said, giving him a quick on the cheek then hurrying to board the train.

Perhaps the Millionaire book is right, Amber thought ruefully. The trick to hooking a millionaire was to not chase after them. It had certainly worked with Randy.

As soon as she got home, Amber contacted a local estate agent and put her flat on the market. She spent the rest of the week tidying the flat, ready for prospective purchasers. Then, that weekend, she drove over to see her parents to tell them of her plans.

As she took the turning off the motorway to the leafy suburb where her parents lived, her mind kept drifting to Jed. What was he doing now? Was he missing her as much as she was missing him? Realising she'd almost missed the turning, she indicated right quickly, causing the car behind to brake hard. The driver tooted the horn loudly at her. Bother, she had to keep her mind on the road or she'd end up having an accident.

A couple more turnings and she was in the quiet lane which led to her parents' detached Tudor house. She drove down the drive and pulled up outside the black and white beamed building. Getting out of the car, she stood there for a moment, looking around at the immaculate lawns and colourful flowerbeds, remembering the happy days of her childhood. It would be difficult living at home again after having her own flat for a few years and coming and going as she pleased. But she would adjust. Her parents loved this house and there was no way she was going to sit back and watch while it was taken from them.

The front door opened and her mother appeared on the doorstep. She smiled and waved at Amber.

'Amber, this is a surprise. How lovely to see you!'

Amber locked the car then walked up the path to greet her mother. 'How are you, Mum? How's Dad?' She kissed her on the cheek, thinking how pale and drawn her mother was. It had been a hard time for her, she knew that, and wished she could have given her more support. She should never have listened to Callie and gone to Coombe Bay. She should have thought of selling her flat before so her parents wouldn't have had all this stress.

'He's much better. He's even been able to do a bit of DIY. But don't take my word for it, come and see for yourself.'

Amber followed her mother into the house and was surprised to see her father putting up a shelf on the wall.

'Hello, love,' He glanced over his shoulder at her. 'Your mum's been getting me to do all the odd jobs I've been promising to do for years. I can't wait to get back to work and have a rest.' He winked at her then turned his attention back to screwing in a wall bracket.

'You look a lot better,' Amber told him.

'And getting fitter every day.' Dad gave the screwdriver a final twist then reached for the other bracket.

'That's good.' Amber smiled at him. 'Just don't do too much or you'll be ill again.'

'I'm fine. No need to worry about me,' he assured her.

'Let's have a cup of tea,' Mum said, unplugging the kettle and taking it over to the sink to fill up. 'Then you can tell us your news, Amber.'

Amber sat down at the huge wooden table which had been in the kitchen for as long as she could remember. She remembered all the birthday parties she'd had around that table, all the family Christmas dinner with her grandparents, aunts, uncles, and cousins. This house held so many happy memories. She wasn't going to let her parents lose it.

'I've come to tell you that you don't have to sell the house and your money worries will soon be over,' she blurted out.

'How's that? Have you won the lottery?' her father asked, screwing the shelf securely onto the brackets.

Her mother sat down in the chair opposite her. 'I hope you haven't done anything silly,' she said.

You don't want to know what I almost did, Mum.

She told them about her plan to sell her flat and move back home. 'Now you can pay of your debts and you won't have to sell up,' she said.

Her parents stared at her, stunned.

'I'm not having you doing that,' her father said when he finally found his voice. 'It's kind of you, but no. I pay my own debts.'

She could see she'd hurt his pride.

'Look, Dad, it was my fault you bought those shares and lost all your money so it's up to me to pay you back.'

'Your fault?' Her father walked over to the table and thumped it with his fist. 'It was nothing to do with you. It was my decision. I was the one who asked Rod about them and I was the one who decided to buy them. I know that shares can go down as well as up and decided to take the risk. It's my fault and no one else's and you are not selling your home to bail me out. Is that understood?'

'Joe, Amber was only trying to help,' Mum reminded him. She looked at Amber. 'It's kind of you, dear, but your dad is right, the last thing we want is for you to sell your home.'

'Then what are you going to do?' Amber asked. 'You've already had the bailiffs here. I don't want you to lose this house. You've lived here all your lives. I grew up here. So did you, Dad, and your family before you.'

'Oh, Amber, I'm sorry. I should never have told you about the bailiffs and worried you so much. I was going to phone you again today and let you know that your father and I have sorted it out. We don't have to sell the house. Let me finish making this cup of tea then we'll tell you all about it.'

Amber smiled in spite of herself as her mother spooned some tea leaves into the pot and poured the boiling water on them. Her mother would insist on making a cup of tea if war was about to break out.

Her father sat down at the table, reached over, and placed his hand on hers. It was rough with short, bitten nails. Workman's hands. Like Jed's. No wonder she hadn't realised he was a millionaire.

Would she never stop thinking about him?

'Sorry, love,' he said, gruffly. 'I didn't mean to fly off the handle like that but I don't want you paying my debts. And it's time you stopped blaming yourself for what Rod did. You picked a bad one when you went out with him but it happens. We all make mistakes.'

'That's what Jed said,' she murmured. *Here I go again.*

'Jed?'

'Oh, just someone I met.'

'Someone special judging by the look in your eyes,' her mother said, placing a cup of tea in front of her and Dad's big, blue mug in front of him.

Very special.

She shrugged. 'Maybe.' She took a sip of the tea. It was too milky, as usual but she tried not to grimace. 'Thanks, Mum. Now tell me about your plan.'

'You tell her, Joe.' Her mother sat down in the chair opposite.

Amber listened as her father explained they were going to turn the top floor of the house into two flats. 'A financial adviser friend talked to us about it. We can take out a second mortgage to cover the costs – the bank has already agreed – and the rent will cover our mortgage payments and leave us some to live on,' he said. 'The house is too big for me and your mother now. Those attic rooms are just lying empty. We might as well make use of them.'

'We'll only let them to professional people, of course,' her mother added. 'We've signed up with a rather exclusive agency and they have people on their books waiting to rent a flat in a place like ours.'

Amber had to admit it seemed the perfect solution.

She hadn't needed her Millionaire Plan after all. Jed was right. Her parents would have been horrified if they'd known she was intending to marry for money just to help them out. How could she have been so stupid as to even consider it? All she'd succeeded in doing is making a fool of herself and losing the only man she had ever truly loved.

Chapter Ten

Rule number 10: Demand an expensive engagement ring and a big wedding. He can afford it and you deserve it.

'Didn't you meet Lord Guy Turner when you were in England?' Chloe asked, looking up from the magazine she was reading as Jed walked into the room. 'I'm sure you mentioned him to me.'

'Yes, why?' he replied. He briefly recalled mentioning going to the party on Lord Guy's yacht when Chloe had pestered him to tell her all about his travels but was surprised that she'd remembered it.

'There's a big spread here about his son's wedding. Honestly, the English and their aristocracy. This guy's famous just because of the family he's been born into, nothing to do with what he's achieved. Mind you, his bride's beautiful. She's pregnant, apparently. Jed ...' She stared at him. 'What's wrong?'

So she'd married him.

For a moment he couldn't speak. He felt winded, as if he'd been punched in the stomach. He'd spend the last few months trying, unsuccessfully, not to think of Amber, throwing himself into his work like a man demented. But she was always there, invading his thoughts, disturbing his peace of mind. A flash of honey brown hair in the street, a tinkling laugh, a glimpse of long, sun-tanned legs clad in denim shorts would all remind him of her. At night, she was there, waiting to visit him in his dreams, kissing him, promising her undying love and he'd wake up longing to see her and hold her once more. Then he'd remember how she'd betrayed him, had only been after him for his money and would harden his heart.

But he still loved her.

And the knowledge that she'd married Randy and was carrying his baby sent him reeling.

You knew she would, he reminded himself. Right from the beginning she'd been totally honest about it '*I need to marry a millionaire,*' she'd said.

The trouble was, she'd neglected to tell him he was the millionaire she had in mind. Perhaps because she didn't know who he was at first, but she lost no time in making a play for him when she found out his true identity. And he fell for it.

'She's the one, isn't she? The one who broke your heart?'

'What?' Chloe's words brought him back to the present. How had she guessed?

Chloe smiled softly. 'You haven't been yourself since you came back, Jed. One minute throwing yourself into your work like a man possessed and the next staring blankly out of the window for hours on end. It's obvious you're upset over a woman. Why did you let her go if you loved her so much?'

'She only wanted to marry me for my money.' He bit the words out. 'Luckily I found out in time.'

Chloe raised an eyebrow. 'So she married this Randy instead? Well, I guess you're well rid. I must say, I'm surprised you fell for another Melissa. It's not like you to get bitten twice.'

'She didn't seem like Melissa. She didn't even look like her.'

Amber, with her honey brown hair, soft fudge brown eyes, petite curvy figure, looked so innocent and honest – the exact opposite of tall, willowy Melissa with her cool, blonde model girl looks and sophisticated manner. Only Amber hadn't been as innocent and honest as he thought, had she?

'She looks like her to me. Same long, blonde hair, same vacuous expression on her face and same fixed smile,' Chloe said, studying the magazine thoughtfully.

Long, blonde hair?

Jed strode across the room, snatched the magazine out of her hands, and stared at the picture of Randy with his arms around a beautiful blonde woman in an expensive wedding dress. Tamara.

So Amber hadn't married him.

'That's not her!' The words were out before he could stop them.

'So you were wrong about her, this woman who broke your heart?' Chloe asked him, looking at him speculatively. 'She wasn't marrying you for your money?'

Had he been wrong? For a moment his heart soared then it came crashing back to earth again. What if she hadn't married Randy? It didn't change anything. She'd still only accepted his proposal because she'd found out he was rich, up until then it was Randy she'd set her sights on. And Randy she'd turned to when Jed had walked out on her. Obviously, something had gone wrong with her plan. Perhaps Randy had decided she wasn't sophisticated enough for him.

He shook his head. 'No, it was definitely my money she was after. She told me when I first met her that she wanted to hook a millionaire.'

Chloe looked surprised. 'Well, that was honest of her. So you knew the score from the beginning?'

'Yes, no ... we ...' Jed found himself telling Chloe everything.

Chloe listened attentively. When he'd finished she was silent for a moment, as if digesting all the information. Then, she tilted her head to one side, tapping her chin with her finger. 'I think you might have misjudged her, Jed,' she said. 'For a start, she might not have even read the magazine. Didn't you say she shared the flat with her friend?'

'It's a bit of a coincidence isn't it, when she'd admitted she was trying to hook a millionaire?'

'Exactly. Why tell you that if she knew you were rich, if she was trying to "hook" you. And why be so honest with you about her plans? It doesn't make sense. And why stuff the magazine down the sofa, knowing you would probably sit there? Why not keep it in her bedroom, out of sight?' Chloe pointed out. 'And if she did see it and she planned to marry you surely she'd have accepted your proposal right away. It seems to me that she fell in love with you in spite of herself. Just like you did to her.'

Jed thought back to the first time he'd met Amber. How unaffected she was, gazing around his yacht in awe, so nervous about doing or saying anything wrong. How she'd confided in him. He would have staked his life it wasn't an act. Could Chloe be right? Had Amber really not known who he was?

'Then why didn't she come and find me and explain?' he demanded. 'Why did she leave with Randy?'

'Perhaps he was giving her a lift to the station. And maybe she didn't try to explain because she was hurt you didn't trust her.'

'*I* didn't trust *her*?' He almost exploded with outrage. 'How did I get to be the villain in all this?'

Chloe folded her arms and titled her head to one side. 'The way I see it, this Amber was honest with you. You've admitted she told you her plans right from the start and asked for your help. But you kept the truth from her. It must have been pretty devastating for her to discover you were loaded, especially when she's so frankly told you she wanted to marry a millionaire. She probably thought you'd never believe her, never trust her again so what was the point of coming after you and trying to explain?'

He was silent, digesting this new train of thought.

'And she must have been angry too. Thinking that you'd taken her for a fool.' Chloe stood up and paced around the room, gesticulating as she talked. 'Think about it. There she was babbling on about trying to marry a millionaire and asking for tips on mixing with the rich, thinking you were a nobody like her and all the while you were a billionaire but didn't let on. She must have thought you were laughing at her, taking her for an idiot.'

Jed raked his hand through his hair. He didn't like how Chloe was twisting this. 'How could I tell her? I wanted her to love me for myself, not my money.'

'I know that, Jed, but look at it from Amber's point of view. She thought you were a friend, she confided in you. Then you both fell in love. You asked her to marry you and she agreed, forgetting her plans even though this Randy was desperate to marry her. Next thing she knows, you've done a runner, leaving her to learn from a magazine article that you're not who you pretended to be.'

'It wasn't like that!' he yelled.

'From where she's standing that's probably exactly what it's like,' Chloe told him.

Jed stared at her. Could she be right?

'Look, Jed, I've never seen you like this over a woman, not even Melissa. If this Amber means so much to you why are you so willing to let her go?'

He digested this in silence. Chloe's words made him take a long hard look at himself and he had to admit she was right. He had lied to Amber, hadn't trusted her with the truth. Why should he? He'd wanted her to marry him for love, not money. But perhaps that's exactly what she had been doing. Perhaps he'd judged her wrong. He thought back to the island, remembered how close they'd been. How right it had felt when he held her in his arms, kissed her. He'd never felt like this about anyone. What if Chloe was right and Amber hadn't known the truth about him? She would have been devastated.

He made a snap decision to go and see her, to find out for his own peace of mind. Not that he knew where she lived, but he knew where Callie's aunt lived and from there he could trace Callie then Amber. If Amber wanted to see him, that was.

'You're right,' he said. 'Can you book me a flight to England as soon as possible? To land in Exeter airport?' He could hire a car from there to drive to Coombe Bay.

Chloe smiled. 'Good for you,' she said. 'And this time don't let her get away.'

The sound of the phone ringing woke Amber from yet another dream of Jed. No matter how much she managed to block him out during the day, and it wasn't easy even now a few months had passed since she last saw him, he always interrupted her dreams. She groaned, glanced at the clock, saw it was only 7.30 and pulled the duvet over her head. Whoever it was could leave a message and wait until a more reasonable time for a Saturday morning chat. She'd had a long, hard week and needed her sleep.

The phone automatically switched to answerphone but no message was left. Then it started ringing again a few minutes later. Amber sighed and reached out for the receiver. 'Hello, Amber Wynter speaking and this had better be good,' she mumbled sleepily.

'Amber.' Callie's voice took her by surprise. Her friend wasn't normally up this time on a Saturday morning. Her next words took Amber's breath away. 'I thought I'd better warn you that Jed's looking for you.'

Jed.

Amber sat up shutting her eyes and gripping the receiver tightly as the memories came flooding back. Jed's smile, his drop-dead sexy face, his caress, his kisses ...

The way he'd deceived her. Walked out without even saying goodbye.

She moistened her lips. 'What does he want?'

'I don't know but he called at Aunt Sophie's yesterday asking if she knew your address, saying he'd lost your phone number and charmed her into giving him mine. Then he phoned last night when I was out and Suzy, my dippy new flatmate, gave him the address of our flat so he's coming to see me this morning. He's bound to ask for your phone number or address. What shall I do?'

In her heart Amber longed to see Jed but she knew it was pointless. They couldn't turn the clock back. Jed hadn't trusted her and he never would. He would always believe she was after him for his money. And she would never forgive him for keeping the truth a secret from her, for letting her think he was something he wasn't. For making a fool of her.

'I don't want to see him, Callie. Don't give him my phone number or address, please,' she begged. She'd changed her mobile phone number some time ago so Randy couldn't contact her – he'd been so persistent. Had Jed been trying to contact her on her mobile?

'Are you sure? You still love him, I know you do. And he's come all the way from America to see you. Maybe you should hear what he's got to say.'

'No.' Amber was determined. 'I never want to see him again.'

'Is that what you want me to tell him?'

'Yes. Tell him to go back to America. He's wasting his time trying to find me. We've got nothing to say to each other.'

'If you're sure it's what you want.' Callie sounded doubtful.

'It is.'

Amber put the phone down, her hand shaking. Why did Jed want to speak to her after all this time? For a while, when her anger at how he'd deceived her had subsided she'd hoped, prayed he would come back to her, try to sort things out, but he hadn't. And now it was too late.

She didn't trust Callie not to give Jed her address. Her friend had made no secret of the fact she thought Amber was wrong and should see him. She'd been telling Amber for ages to write to Jed and explain what had happened. And Jed could be charming when he wanted to be, look how he'd charmed Callie's aunt and her flatmate into giving him information. So she decided it was best if she went away to visit her parents for the weekend, just in case Jed came calling. Hopefully, if he did turn up and found she wasn't there he'd go back to America and leave her alone.

If I set out now I'll be there by nine, she thought, throwing back the duvet and heading for the shower. Her parents were early risers so she knew they'd be up and delighted to see her. She'd invent some excuse for arriving so early, perhaps ask her mother to come on a shopping trip with her. Anything was better than coming face to face with Jed again. It had taken her months to put him to the back of her mind and get on with her life. She knew she couldn't cope with seeing him again.

Amber was delighted to see her parents looking so relaxed and happy. Her father was now back in work, their debts were paid off and the top floor flats were almost ready. Apparently they had tenants already waiting to move in. She had been stupid to think she had to marry a millionaire to help them, she thought as she sat in the kitchen, sipping a cup of tea while she waited for her mother to get ready for their shopping trip. If only Callie hadn't come up with that wild scheme she would never have met Jed and would have been spared a lot of heartache.

Did she really wish she'd never met Jed? At least now she knew what real love was. What she'd felt for Rod had been nothing compared to the feeling she'd had – still had – for Jed. What was that old cliché? It was better to have loved and lost than never to have loved at all.

'You look miles away, love. Are you OK?' her father asked.

Amber gave him a reassuring smile. 'Fine, thanks, Dad. I was just thinking how good is was to see you fit again, and you and Mum looking so happy.'

Her father's face was etched with concern. 'I wish I could say the same for you. You've been looking so peaky the past few months. Are you sure nothing's worrying you?'

'I'm fine, Dad, Honest. Just working a bit hard,' she reassured him.

Thankfully, her mother than appeared, ready to go shopping, and saved her from further questioning.

They had a good day. Amber bought herself a new top and persuaded her mother to buy a camel skirt that she loved but was worried might be too young for her, then treated her to lunch at a café.

'Is it a man?' her mother asked as they tucked into cheese omelettes and salad.

'Is what a man?' Amber pretended to be puzzled although she knew perfectly well what her mother was talking about.

'You're not sleeping or eating properly and the sparkle has gone out of your eyes,' her mother replied. 'That usually means man trouble. Is it finished for good?'

'Completely dead and buried,' Amber admitted.

'That's a shame. It would be nice for you to find someone else,' her mother said. She sighed. 'Are you sure there's no chance of you making up?'

'None at all.' Amber half-heartedly, pushed the omelette around her plate. 'So please can we change the subject?'

Her mother gave her a sympathetic look but didn't probe any further and started to relate some family gossip.

After the meal they resumed their shopping, finally arriving aback at six thirty. They showed her father what they'd bought – which included a new shirt and book on fishing for him – then settled down to eat dinner and watch TV. Amber found it hard to concentrate, her mind kept drifting to Jed, wondering what he wanted to see her about and whether he'd persuaded Callie to give him her address or phone number. She'd deliberately switched off her mobile so no one could contact her and find out where she was.

'Are you all right, dear?' her mother asked. 'You look miles away.'

Amber yawned and glanced at the clock. It was almost ten thirty. She knew her parents would be turning in pretty soon. 'Just a bit tired, that's all,' she said. 'I think I'll pop up now. Good night'

'How about some hot chocolate before you go?' her mother asked. 'I've got some marshmallows.'

Would hot chocolate and marshmallows always remind her of Jed? 'Thanks, Mum, that'd be lovely. I'll take it up with me, if you don't mind.'

'Of course not. Tell you what, you go and get ready and I'll bring it up.'

I feel like I've regressed to being a child again. Amber thought, as she sat in her childhood bedroom reading and sipping hot chocolate, two pink marshmallows melting on the top. Still, it was nice to be back home and cosseted for a while. It made her feel safe and secure. Jed couldn't hurt her here.

The next morning was a lovely, crisp autumn day so she set off across the meadow for a walk. She passed a dog barking happily as it chased the falling leaves and her thoughts drifted to Tess. She wondered how Tess and Mike the warden were doing. She'd enjoyed the time she spent on Blyte Island with Jed. Stolen time, like nothing else had mattered but the two of them. When Jed had just been Jed Curtess the wildlife photographer and millionaire's hired help, not Jed Curtess, American property tycoon and hotshot billionaire. She'd loved him so much. Still did if she was honest. And now he was back in England and looking for her. Why?

Whatever the reason was she knew she didn't want to – couldn't – see him. It would hurt too much.

After an hour or so she set off back, feeling calmer and stronger. There was no need for her to run away like this. She didn't have to talk to Jed even if he turned up at her flat. She just wouldn't answer the door, he'd soon get the message and leave her alone. It was hardly likely he'd come all the way to England just to see her, anyway, he was probably on business and decided to look her up while he was here.

Why would he want to do that after the way they'd parted?

As she walked up the drive she noticed a sleek black BMW parked outside the house. Her parents obviously had company. She didn't fancy making polite conversation so decided to go straight to her room and leave them to it.

'You've got a visitor, Amber,' her mother called as Amber opened the door. 'He'd travelled all the way from America to see you.'

America?

Jed!

'Hello, Amber.' Jed came out of the lounge and her heart flipped. 'It's good to see you.'

She stared at him dumbfounded. What was he doing here? She opened her mouth to speak but no words would come out so she shut it again quickly.

'Surprised to see me, eh?' he asked softly.

She found her voice but it came out in a squeak. 'You could say that.'

Her father glanced from one to the other. 'Jed said you were old friends.'

Friends? She thought they had been a bit more than that.

'Perhaps we could go for a drink,' Jed suggested. 'We've got a lot of catching up to do.'

She didn't want to go for a drink with him, but she didn't want to talk to him here, in front of her parents either. It would be too awkward. So she agreed.

'I guess Callie gave you this address even though I told her not to let you know where I lived?' she asked as she got into his car.

'She took some persuading, but she finally gave me the address of your flat. When I arrived and found you gone she guessed you'd gone to your parents so gave me their address too.' He fastened his seat belt and switched on the engine. 'Your parents are nice and your father tells me he's back at work now.'

'Sounds like you had a good chat whilst you waited for me!' she snapped. 'Fished out what information you could, I suppose. Found out whether I'd married a millionaire or not.'

He checked his mirrors then pulled away from the kerb. 'Can we discuss this when we get to the pub, please?' he asked, calmly. 'I like to keep my attention on the road when I'm driving. Especially as I'm used to driving on the other side of the road.'

She threw him a scathing look but said nothing. Actually, it was a relief to have an excuse to be silent for a while, give her chance to get her jumbled emotions in order. She couldn't believe Jed had actually tracked her down. And that she was reacting in the usual way to his presence. She'd hoped she'd got over him but the way her nerves were tingling all over warned her she was still attracted to him. What did he want?

It wasn't until they were seated at a secluded table in the village pub, each with half a pint of shandy in front of them, that she plucked up the courage to ask him.

'What do you want? Why are you here?' she asked, forcing herself to meet his eye. Her heart flipped, as she knew it would.

'I wanted to see you. To apologise,' he told her.

'Apologise?' It was the last thing she expected to hear.

'Yes. For running off like that. It was unforgivable of me. I should have given you chance to explain but when I saw the article I thought ...'

'I know exactly what you thought.' She couldn't keep the bitterness out of her voice. 'That it was you I was after all along. That I'd agreed to marry you because you were rich. That I was after your money.'

His eyes never left hers. 'Yes,' he agreed.

'Well, you were wrong. I didn't know. I had never seen the magazine. Simon brought it home to show Callie when I was out with you.' She swallowed. 'He'd thought he recognised you but couldn't think why. Callie put it behind the cushion so she could show me later.'

'I know. She told me. She wanted to see your face when you found out the man you loved was a millionaire.'

Her throat felt dry. 'Why have you come back to apologise now? It's been eighteen weeks.' *Oh, that's right, Amber. Let him know you've been counting.*

'And four days,' he added solemnly.

She stared at him, uncomprehendingly. What did he want?

He took a sip of his shandy. 'I came back the next morning, you know. I couldn't sleep all night. I wanted to believe that you hadn't read the article, to give you chance to explain. As I arrived I saw you leaving with Randy. He was carrying your suitcase.'

'And you thought I'd moved onto him seeing as you'd sussed out my plan?' She stared at him incredulously. How could he believe she was so ruthless? So mercenary?

He had the grace to look embarrassed. 'It seemed logical at the time.'

'I expect it did seeing as I'd confessed to being a gold digger,' she replied, bitterly. 'So what made you decide you might be wrong about me?'

'I saw – or rather my sister did – an article about Randy and Tamara's wedding. That's when I realised you hadn't married him.'

'Yes, Tamara was making a play for you, you know, but when you left she and Randy decided to join forces.' Then she realised what he'd said. 'Your sister knows about me?'

'A little. She could tell I wasn't myself when she came back and guessed that "woman trouble" was the reason.'

'Like my mum.' She couldn't help but smile.

'She told me I should come and find you, give you a chance to explain. That a woman who was so totally honest as to admit to me that she was looking for a millionaire to marry – and for such honourable reasons as yours – didn't sound the sort of woman who would be so deceitful. She was convinced you hadn't read the article, that you would have asked me about it if you had. Actually, she said you'd have been mad at me.'

Too true she would have. 'Nice that someone had faith in me.'

'I'm sorry,' he said, softly. 'But you must admit it looked black.'

She nodded thoughtfully. 'I know, but I'd always been honest with you. I wouldn't have – couldn't have – pretended I loved you just so I could marry you for your money. I thought you knew me better than that.'

'We don't actually know each other though, do we?' Jed pointed out. 'We only had a few days together and our feelings took over. We didn't have chance to gather our thoughts, we were just swept up by our emotions. At least that's what it was like for me.'

'Me too,' she admitted.

They both sipped their drinks in silence for a moment, digesting the things they'd learnt, the feelings they'd admitted for each other.

'So why didn't you marry Randy? Callie said he'd begged you too.'

'Because I loved you,' she said simply. 'Marrying Randy when I thought I would never love again, when we were both doing it as a business arrangement was fine. At least, it seemed it. But marrying him when I loved someone else was wrong. I couldn't do it.'

'What about helping your parents?'

She told him how she'd planned to sell her flat and move it with them but her parents wouldn't hear of it and were turning the top floor into flats instead.

'So that's why you accepted my proposal? You'd worked out another way to help your parents out?'

'Yes. Marrying a millionaire was a dumb idea of Callie's. I should never have gone along with it. I doubt if I would have been able to carry it through. I was just so worried about Dad and desperate to help I wasn't thinking straight.'

He reached out and took her hand, caressing it gently, sending shivers up her arm, down her spine, making her knees turn to jelly.

'Well now we've sorted everything out we can go back to how we were, can't we?'

'What do you mean?'

'We can get married. Like we were going to.'

Get married? He couldn't be serious.

She pulled her hand away from his. 'No we can't. I can't marry you!'

'Why not? You love me, I know you do. And I love you.'

'Because you aren't the man I thought you were. You're not Jed Curtess the hired hand of a millionaire and part-time wildlife photographer. You're Jed Curtess, American billionaire and property dealer.'

'What difference does that make?' he asked, bewildered.

'Maybe none if you'd been straight with me at the beginning' She stood up and gathered her coat and bag. 'Only you weren't honest with me, were you? You didn't trust me enough to tell me the truth.' She forced herself to keep her voice calm. 'That's the reason I didn't come after you and try to explain about the article, Jed. Because you deceived me. I was honest with you but you didn't trust me enough to be honest with me. And if we got married it would always be there in the background. You'd always be wondering if I married you for your money.'

'I wouldn't,' he protested, standing up.

'Yes, you would,' she told him. 'You might not want to but you wouldn't be able to help yourself.'

Then without as much as a backward glance she walked out.

Chapter Eleven

Jed's Rules: If you love her, fight for her.

She's right, Jed realised. He was the one who had been dishonest, not her. He hadn't trusted her. He'd lied to her whereas she had always been completely honest with him. He now knew beyond any shadow of doubt that she wasn't after his money. On the contrary, it was the knowledge he was a billionaire that was preventing her from marrying him. She loved him. He could see it in her eyes, hear it in her voice. He would never, ever wonder if she had married him for his money. But she would always think he did. Like she said, it would always hang between them.

He ordered a soft drink and sat nursing it while he considered what to do next. He wanted to go after Amber, ask her to change her mind but he was worried if he followed her back to her parents' house she would refuse to see him. He tried to think what Chloe would advise him to do. 'If you love her, fight for her,' she'd urged him as he left. The trouble was, he didn't know how to fight for a woman. He'd never had to too. Women had always chased him, fallen at his feet, been eager to fall into his arms. Amber had never done that. He'd judged her as if she was one of the scheming gold-diggers that always hung around the haunts of millionaires yet he'd known deep in his heart she was different. Only he'd been too scared to trust his heart, too scared of getting hurt. And now he'd lost her.

Amber didn't want to go straight home and face her parents. She knew Jed had managed to charm them and now they were convinced he was a thoroughly nice young man, ideal for her to settle down with. If only. Tears filled her eyes and she turned away from the village, over to the meadow where she'd walked earlier that morning. It had upset her far more than she'd thought it would to see Jed again. She'd worked hard over the past few months to put him out of her mind and get on with her life but as soon as she saw him again the old feelings came flooding back. She longed to run back to the pub, into his arms, tell him she loved him and would marry him but she knew it would never work. Their marriage would be doomed before it even started.

She walked for ages, remembering the good times she'd shared with Jed, their kisses, wondering how she'd ever get over him. Would the pain ever stop?

Her mother took one look at her face when she returned home and hugged her. 'You never sorted it out then, whatever it is that's keeping you two apart.'

She shook her head, miserably. 'It's too big to sort, Mum.'

'Nothing is insurmountable if you love someone,' her mother told her. 'You'll find a way if you're meant to be together.'

Mum and her homespun philosophy, Amber thought. If only life was so simple.

She drove home after lunch, thinking of her mother's words but no matter how hard she thought and how much she wanted to, she couldn't find a way to be with Jed. His money and the knowledge he'd lied to her was too big an obstacle to get over.

Callie was on the phone as soon as Amber arrived home, explaining why she'd given Jed her parents' address and wanting to know what had happened. She told Amber she'd been trying to contact her on her mobile all weekend.

'I switched it off in case you'd given Jed my number

and he tried to phone me,' Amber explained. She only just realised that it was still switched off and had turned it back on again a few minutes ago.

'Did you see him? How did it go?' Callie asked, eagerly.

Amber told her.

'You're mad,' her friend declared. 'You love him and he loves you. You're meant to be together.'

'It isn't enough,' Amber replied. 'We need to trust each other too. Jed will always wonder if I married him for his money, and I'll always know he's wondering that. It will destroy us.'

'You turned Randy down and you've turned Jed down twice,' Callie said slowly, as if she was explaining a simple fact to an idiot. 'How could he possibly think you were marrying him for his money? It's because of his money that you aren't marrying him.'

'What do you mean?'

'Well, if he wasn't so stinking rich you'd marry him tomorrow, wouldn't you?'

'It's not just that he's loaded, Callie. He kept it secret from me. He didn't trust me enough to tell me.'

'And if he had told you, would you have married him?'

She thought about it. 'No,' she said, slowly.

'I rest my case,' Callie sounded triumphant. 'You're letting the fact that Jed is rich keep you apart. You're punishing the guy for something he can't do anything about. Unless you want him to give all his money away, of course.'

Callie was right, Amber thought, as she tossed and turned in her bed that night. She wouldn't marry Jed because he was rich. No other reason. She accepted his proposal when she thought he was a poor photographer. OK, he was the one who'd walked away but as soon as she'd found out the truth about him she would have called the wedding off. Maybe she was stupid, stubborn, and all the other things Callie had said before she finally put down the phone, but she loved Jed too much to risk it going wrong. And the way she saw it, the stakes were against a happy marriage.

Monday morning, after another sleepless night, things didn't seem so cut and dried. She loved Jed. He loved her. He'd come all the way from America to try and sort things out but she'd sent him packing. Was she crazy?

I had no choice, she told herself as she got ready for work. He's an American billionaire. Even if he did trust her, and she wasn't convinced he did, their lives were too different. She'd never fit into his world. And he must have realised it too because he'd made no attempt to contact her since yesterday lunchtime. Obviously, he'd gone back to America, his mind at peace because he'd talked to her and tried to sort it out. In fact, it was probably only guilt about the way he'd treated her which had made him look her up in the first place. After all, he hadn't tried too hard to talk her around, had he?

It was a long day. Unable to concentrate, Amber made countless mistakes, including deleting a client's file which she'd been working on the previous week. Helen, her boss, finally sent her home and told her to stop there until she'd sorted herself out.

'Either win him back or put him out of your head,' Helen advised.

Easier said than done.

Callie phoned her later that evening. 'Have you heard from him?' she asked.

Amber didn't need to ask who she was on about. 'Of course not, he's gone back home now. He only wanted to see me to clear his conscience.'

'Do I detect a note of regret that you sent him packing?'

Yes. 'I had to, Callie. There's no way we could have made it work.'

'I've got his mobile number if you want to call him. He might not have gone back yet.'

Amber paused. Did she?

'Amber?'

'No, it's best this way.' If he'd have truly loved her, meant what he said, he'd have tried a bit harder to win her back. Phoned her to see if she'd changed her mind. Come around again. Sent flowers. Anything to show he cared.

'OK, but I think you're making a big mistake,' Callie told her. 'You two are made for each other. You're just too stubborn to admit it.'

Amber spent the evening thinking about Jed and came to the conclusion that, as much as it hurt, she'd done the right thing. What's more, she was relieved that Jed had accepted her decision and gone back home. Now she had to put it behind her and get on with her life.

She returned to work next day, focused and determined. By lunchtime she'd got the client file back on the computer and was working on a brilliant graphic design.

'Excellent work,' Helen told her. 'So you managed to sort things out with him then?'

'No but I've put him out of my head,' Amber replied.

She'd spent enough time crying over Jed. It was time to move on. So when a group from the office invited her to join them for drinks after work, she agreed. She could only have soft drinks as she'd driven to work but she was socialising again instead of living like a recluse. Jed was gone forever. She had to accept it. He'd apologised, asked her marry him again, she'd refused, he'd gone home. End of story.

She had a great evening and didn't think of Jed at all. Well, hardly at all. Only every five minutes or so. And the reason she dashed to the phone as soon as she returned home to check her messages was in case anyone important had phoned her.

Like Jed.

No one had phoned at all. Especially not Jed. Incredible that it still hurt how easily he'd walked away from her.

Get over it, Amber. Jed has. He's put you out of his life.

When she arrived home from work the following evening, Jed's BMW was parked outside the block of flats.

He'd come back.

Her heart did a somersault as he got out of the car and walked towards her, looking so handsome and knee-jerkingly sexy that her bones felt like they'd been turned to jelly.

'I thought you'd have gone back to America by now,' she said, hoping her voice didn't sound as breathless as she felt.

'I can't go back yet. I haven't followed all the plan.'

She stared at him, confused. 'What plan?'

'The "how to hook Amber" plan,' he said solemnly. 'My sister helped me work it out.'

'Your sister?' Honestly, she was beginning to sound like a parrot.

'Yes, we worked it out before I came over to find you. When you walked out the pub on Sunday I thought maybe I should give up and go back home but I couldn't. Not without seeing the plan through.' He took a piece of paper out of his pocket. 'Let me see, I'm on rule number five.'

Then before she realised what he was planning he stepped forward, drew her in his arms, and kissed her. Deeply, passionately, hungrily. And despite herself she was responding, running her fingers through his hair, pressing her body against his, returning kiss for exquisite kiss.

'Wow!' he said shakily, gently pulling away. 'Does that mean you're pleased to see me?'

She stared at him, trying to control her ragged breathing, not trusting herself to speak. Why did he always have this effect on her?

Because you love him. Why keep fighting it?

Who said she could fight it?

'Shall we go inside?' he suggested, glancing over his shoulder. 'There's a couple of curtains twitching in the block of flats and I don't want to sully your reputation with the neighbours.'

She nodded numbly as he placed his arm around her, sending her senses reeling again, and gently led her inside.

'What were rules one to four?' she asked when she finally found her voice.

Jed guided her into the lift, his arm still around her waist, and spun her around to face him as the lift doors closed.

'Rule number one was to come back to England and find you.' He kissed her on the forehead. 'Number two was to apologise for the way I walked out on you and to give you a chance to explain.' He kissed her on the tip of her nose. 'Number three was to tell you I love you,' He kissed her on her left cheek. 'Number four was to do all the running and not let you get away.' He kissed her on her right cheek. 'And number five is to kiss you.' He kissed her soundly on the lips.

She groaned, entwined her arms around his neck, and gave into the wild, uncontrollable urge to kiss him back.

The lift doors opened and someone coughed. Loudly. Amber opened her eyes and saw Mrs Gibson, the little old lady from the flat next door smiling at her. She felt her cheeks burn with embarrassment. How could she have got so carried away she hadn't even noticed the lift doors open?

Jed tenderly disentangled her arms from around his neck, and, his arm still wrapped around her waist, guided her out of the lift. 'So sorry, madam. I have asked Amber to exercise some restraint but she just can't resist me,' he told Mrs Gibson.

Amber groaned and buried her face in the sleeve of his jacket.

'Was rule number six to show me up in front of my neighbours?' she asked, taking the key out of her pocket as they reached her flat door.

Jed took the key off her, unlocked the door, gently pushed her inside, then kicked the door shut behind them. 'No, rule six is to make you listen to me,' he said, kissing her again. 'And you're not allowed to interrupt until I've finished.'

'How many rules are there?' she asked

'Only seven,' he said. 'But rule six is the toughest of the lot and the one Chloe insisted is the most important.'

She nodded. 'OK.' She walked over to the sofa and sat down. 'I'm listening.'

Jed sat down beside her. 'Chloe said if I told you about myself you might understand why I misjudged you and realise that, if you take away the trimmings, I am just the simple photographer you fell in love with.'

'That makes sense,' she said cautiously, wondering what dark secrets he was going to come out with.

'I told you about my mother and how she struggled to bring me – and later, Chloe – up single handed,' he said, placing his arm around her shoulder and pulling her closer to him. She rested her head on his chest and listened to his soft American drawl.

'When I was a kid I decided that somehow I was going to get rich and care for my mom, make sure she never had to work again.' His voice was little more than a whisper, as if he was still in the past, remembering those hard times. 'I figured the best way to do that was buy and sell property. So when I left school I worked days in an estate agent's office as a general run around and nights in a bar until I'd earned enough for the deposit on my first house. A run-down place in the town.'

He hugged her tighter as if wanting to make sure she was still there. 'I got a loan to do it up, doing as much of the work as I could myself and sold it at a profit within six months. Then I did the same again. And again. When I'd made enough to buy two properties I did them up, rented one out, and sold the other one at a profit. Within a couple of years I had a string of properties which were bringing in a decent income.'

She smiled at him encouragingly, not wanting to interrupt.

'I bought my mom a lovely little house in the best end of town, and persuaded her to give up work,' he continued. 'Then I got lucky. Thanks to a new shopping mall the prices of my property soared. A couple of years later I was a millionaire.'

She could only guess at how hard he'd worked, holding down two jobs and restoring his run-down properties to make it happen. 'Your mother must have been so proud.'

'She was.' His voice was grim. 'But I forgot about her, Amber. I got so caught up in making money, giving her material things that I forgot she needed my company too. Sometimes I didn't visit her from one month to the next. I was too busy accumulating my fortune. Making sure she never went without again.'

She lifted her head from his shoulder and winced at the raw pain she saw in his eyes, 'I'm sure she understood,' she reassured him, gently tracing her finger across his cheek.

He seized her hand and held it in his, gazing at her for a moment before continuing. 'Mom never complained. It wasn't her nature. She always greeted me with a smile, never reproached me for not visiting. It was Chloe who did that. She visited Mom regular and kept telling me Mom needed my company more than my money. But I was too possessed with making money, scared stiff of being poor again. I just wanted to give my mom the best of everything. I kept promising to visit after the next business meeting, then the next. And when I did visit her I was always preoccupied. Then Chloe phoned me to say Mom had cancer.'

'Oh, Jed.' Her heart went out to him.

'The doctor told us she'd waited too long for treatment. She was living on borrowed time. So, I left someone running the business, bought the yacht – it's named after her, you know, Chenoa means White Dove in Cherokee – and took Mom, and a qualified nurse, sailing around the world. Something she'd always wanted to do.'

He paused and she knew he was trying to deal with his memories. 'We had a great time. I've never seen Mom so happy. I took her to Australia, Africa, China and Japan, then Europe. Chloe flew out to join us whenever she could, with her husband and children. We were on our way to England when Mom fell ill again so we turned back. Two days after we arrived home she died.'

As she listened to him, Amber had a glimpse of that determined little boy vowing that his mother would never know poverty again. Of Jed, the man, working all hours of the day and night, building his business empire so his mum would never do without. She could feel his despair when he found out his beloved mother was dying. *He understands*, she realised suddenly. *He understands why I was willing to marry a millionaire to help my parents. He thought I was wrong, but he understands why I was doing it.*

'When Mom died, I went through a bad patch,' Jed continued, his voice flat. 'That's when Melissa moved in on me, offering me love and sympathy, pretending she was interested in me for myself and not my money. I found out just in time what a gold-digger she was. And disillusioned with a life in pursuit of wealth, with mixing with people who were only interested in me because of my bank balance I decided to take time out. To find out what I wanted to do with my life. So I put a couple of good men in charge of my business and set off in my yacht to sail around the world, alone this time. That's when I got interested in birds. The feathered kind.'

He kissed her forehead. 'You see so many of them out at sea and I realised what fascinating creatures they are. I started taking photographs of them and sending them to magazines. The kick I got when my first photos were published in a nature magazine was almost as big as the one I got when I made my first million. I knew it was what I wanted to do with my life.'

'So when I came along and told you I wanted to hook a millionaire you thought I was just like Melissa and the other hangers-on you'd turned your back on? '

He shook his head. 'No, I knew you were different. You were so honest, so naïve. I was just scared of how you would change if you married someone just for money, that'd you turn bitter, shallow, and twisted like the others, which is why I tried to talk you out of your mad scheme. At least, I thought that was the reason. Later I realised it was because I loved you. That I'd loved you from the first moment I saw you. That's why I was scared to tell you who I was because I wanted someone to love me for me, not for what I had.' He traced her lips with his finger. 'I'm sorry.'

She could understand it clearly now. 'It's OK, I don't blame you,' she told him. 'I shouldn't have been so stupid as to think of marrying someone for their money. It was cold and selfish of me. You must have thought I was completely ruthless.'

'Never,' he said, planting a feather-light kiss on her shoulder. 'But I knew you desperately wanted to help your parents and wasn't quite sure how far you'd go.'

'So what's the last rule?' she asked, shivering as he covered her shoulders then her throat with kisses.

'To buy you the best engagement ring I can find and have a big, posh wedding,' he told her. 'Those are Chloe's orders.'

'That's the one rule our plans agree on,' she told him.

'It's the final rule of the Millionaire Plan.' She smiled at him. 'Do you know something? I broke most of the rules and still managed to hook you. '

'Which just shows we were meant to be together.' He pulled her down beside him, hugging her to him, and rolled them both onto their sides so they were facing each other.

'I think we were,' she agreed, kissing her way up his throat.

'Does that mean you'll marry me?' His tawny eyes held hers, and she saw the love shining through them.

Her heart filled with happiness and love for him. He did trust her or he wouldn't have come looking for her. Why should he? He could have his pick of women. But money can't buy love and he wanted her love.

'Amber?' He cupped her cheek in his hand. 'Will you marry me?'

'Yes,' she whispered. 'Yes, please!'

'Thank you, sweetheart,' he murmured, holding her tight and kissing her, sweetly, slowly, deeply.

For a few moments, they lay in silence, wrapped in each other's arms, content to just hold each other.

'Happy?' Jed mumbled against her ear.

Ecstatic.

'Very,' she said, nudging up even closer to him.

'It seems both of our plans worked,' Jed teased, stroking her hair. 'You got your millionaire and I got you.'

She smiled at him. 'We both forgot to plan what happens after we get married,' she said.

'You're right.' He kissed her forehead. 'Well, you made ten rules so I've got three more rules to make. Let me see,' he thought for a moment then smiled. 'Rule eight is to have a long, exotic honeymoon. And rule nine is to choose a lovely new home to live in.'

'And rule ten?'

'That's easy,' he told her, his eyes brimming with love.

'To live happily ever after.'
   'That,' she replied softy, 'is the best rule of all.'

THE END

Free extract from

The Cornish Hotel by the Sea

Karen King

Chapter One

Ellie jumped as a horn blasted out behind her. Drat, the lights had turned green. As she took off the handbrake and slid into gear the horn blared again. Talk about impatient.

She pulled away, shooting a quick glance in the mirror at the car behind. A sleek silver Mercedes with a dark haired suited guy at the wheel. That figured. Some arrogant, aggressive businessman off to an important meeting no doubt, annoyed at losing a nanosecond because Ellie had been so busy worrying about her mum she hadn't noticed the lights change.

Mum would be okay. She had to be. Ellie couldn't lose her as well. The pain of her dad's death two years ago was still pretty raw.

Ellie bit her lip as she recalled the phone call from Mandy just as she was about to leave for work that morning. She'd known as soon as she'd seen Mandy's number flash up that something was wrong. Mandy was the receptionist at Gwel Teg, the small family hotel that had been Ellie's home until she'd moved to the

Midlands a few years ago, wanting more than the sleepy seaside town of Port Medden offered.

And to get away from Lee and Zoe's betrayal.

"Mandy, is Mum okay?" she'd stammered anxiously.

"Now I don't want you to worry dear …"

Ellie felt the colour drain from her face as she listened to Mandy tell her that her mum had been rushed into Truro hospital early that morning with a bad bout of pleurisy.

"Is she very ill? I'll drive down straight away." Ellie threw back the duvet and was out of bed in a shot.

"You mustn't worry, she'll be fine. You know how tough your mum is," Mandy sounded reassuring. "Don't get rushing, lovey. I don't want you haring down the motorway and having an accident."

"Do you have the phone number of the hospital? What ward is Mum in?"

Ellie grabbed a pen and scribbled the number down on the back of her hand, said goodbye to Mandy then telephoned the hospital.

"Mrs Truman is as comfortable as can be expected," the nurse on the other end of the phone told her.

Which could mean just about anything. So Ellie had immediately packed a case, phoned up work and explained she needed to take a couple of days off – luckily, she was due to take her two weeks holiday on Monday - then set off for the long drive to Cornwall.

She should have visited more often, she reprimanded herself. Mum had sounded so tired the last few times she'd spoken to her, although she insisted she was fine. That's why Ellie had planned to drive down to Cornwall tomorrow evening, straight after work, to spend her holiday helping out at Gwel Teg.

I should have realised it was too much for Mum. I should have gone back to live with her when Dad died.

She was here at last. Turning into the hospital car park, she looked for an empty space. Damn, there was only one place left and it was going to take some very careful reversing to get in to it. She gritted her teeth and manoeuvred very slowly.

It took three attempts but she finally squeezed into the narrow parking bay. She glanced over her shoulder half expecting to see Merc Guy watching in amusement but thankfully no one was around.

A few minutes later she was rushing into the hospital ward.

"Mrs Truman's very poorly at the moment so don't be too shocked how she looks," the nurse on duty said when Ellie introduced herself. "She should pick up in a day or two though. We're lucky we caught her in time."

Ellie *was* shocked to see how pale and thin her mum was. She barely recognised the drained, gaunt face with dark shadows under sunken eyes, framed by short wispy dark hair streaked with grey – very unusual for her mum who reached for the bottle of hair colour at any sign of grey. Her cotton pyjamas hung loosely on her, emphasising her slender frame. She seemed so frail and fragile. And much weaker and older than she'd looked at Christmas, when Ellie had last seen her. That was six months ago, she scolded herself. She should have made the effort to come down more. After all, she was an only child and all the family Mum had left now.

"Hello, love." Sue Truman smiled weakly. "You shouldn't have rushed down to see me. You were coming down tomorrow evening, anyway."

"I wanted to make sure you were all right," Ellie said softly, sitting down besides the bed and gently squeezing her mum's hand. "Mandy's call gave me quite a scare."

"I told her not to bother you," Sue said. A harsh bout of coughing overcome her and she struggled to sit up. Ellie helped her, reaching over to plump up the pillows behind her mum's back for support. "That's a bad cough, Mum."

Sue waved her hand dismissively. "I'm fine, dear," she croaked, between coughs." I'll be out of here in no time."

She didn't look fine, Ellie thought worriedly. "You stay as long as you need, Mum. Just concentrate on getting better. I'll look after the hotel," she promised.

"Nonsense, dear. It's your holiday…" Sue protested feebly.

"I've come down to look after you," Ellie told her

firmly. "And that's what I'm going to do."

She should never have left Mum to cope alone, Ellie thought as she headed off for Port Medden. She should have moved back in and helped.

The sun was out in force now so she was glad of her sunglasses to dull the glare. She wound down her window, loving the feel of the soft wind blowing through her hair as she drove along the winding country lanes, her foot hovering over the brake, ready to stop if something shot around the corner. The hedges were a riot of tiny purple and blue flowers, the air filled with birdsong. She felt her heart lift as the narrow lanes gave way to open fields scattered with grazing cows and frolicking sheep until finally she could see the sun dancing on the ocean in the distance.

You offered to move back in, Mum didn't want you to, she reminded herself.

When Dad had died, Ellie had tried to persuade Mum to sell up and move to the Midlands, where she could keep an eye on her. But Sue had steadfastly refused. She loved Gwel Teg, it was her life, and kept her busy. "I don't want to sit in a little bungalow twiddling my thumbs all day," she said firmly. "Your dad and I spent some happy years here and I intend to keep the place up and running."

Ellie's offer to move in with her had also been

stubbornly refused. "I'm not that old and doddering that I need my daughter to look after me!" Sue had retorted.

So, knowing that her mum loved the hotel, and thinking that maybe it was good for her to have a purpose in life – and to be honest not really wanting to live in the remote Cornish town again - Ellie had returned to her flat in the Midlands. She'd phoned her mum regularly and visited as much as she could - but not often enough by the look of things.

The insistent honking of a horn jolted her to the present. Drat, she'd been so preoccupied with her worries about Mum that she'd turned into Gwel Teg's car park without noticing the car coming out. She frowned. It was that silver Merc again. The guy behind the wheel was impatiently gesturing her to move back, she held up her hand in apology and reversed to let him out. He threw her a cutting glance as he passed then shot off. *Charming! I hope he isn't staying at the hotel.* An awkward customer was the last thing she needed.

"Ellie, lovey!" Mandy came around the front of the desk and gave Ellie a warm hug wrapped in her trademark *Sexy Lady* perfume. "Have you been to see your mum? How is she?"

Mandy had worked at the hotel so long she was more of a friend than an employee. With her bleached blonde hair, red lipstick and flamboyant clothes she was often taken for a bit of an airhead but she was a big-hearted woman who would help anyone.

"Recovering well the nurse said. But Mandy, she looks so weak, so tired."

"Oh lovey. The hotel's too much for her. I've been trying to get her to rest up a bit, but you know your mum, stubborn as a mule." Mandy's heavily mascaraed eyes were full of concern. "I help her a much as I can but…"

Ellie nodded. "I know. I should have come down more often. I could have helped at weekends."

Mandy wagged a finger at her. "Now don't you start guilt-tripping yourself. You've got work and your own life, you can't make a trip from the Midlands every weekend." She stepped back and cast her eyes over Ellie's face. "You look tired. It's been a long journey for you. Why don't you go and freshen up and have something to eat? I can hold the fort here a bit longer."

A freshen up and cup of coffee was exactly what she needed. "Thanks, Mandy. When's Susie due to take over?"

"Susie left a couple of months ago, lovey. Me and your mum manage the reception between us now."

That surprised her. Mum had always hired two receptionists and helped out herself when necessary. Why hadn't she replaced Susie?

And that meant Mandy had been looking after reception since she'd phoned this morning so must have already completed her shift. "Then it's time you went home. Give me half an hour and I'll take over from you," she promised.

"Take your time, there's no rush," Mandy replied but Ellie was already wheeling her suitcase over to the door that led to the private quarters.

The previous owners had converted the left wing of the hotel into an apartment for their personal use, so that's where Ellie and her parents lived. It was bright, airy and spacious. There was a dining kitchen, lounge and two bedrooms, one of them an ensuite, a bathroom and an attic room with an ensuite - which Ellie had fallen in love with as soon as she'd seen it and immediately claimed as hers. She'd adored the sloping roof, the white shutters on the window, and best of all the view over the rooftops to the beach.

The name Gwel Teg – Cornish for 'beautiful view' - suited the hotel. The view from the back was breathtaking, stretching over the cobbled streets of the quaint former fishing town right down to the beach and harbour. Situated about halfway up the hill, with a side-view over to the shops and main beach, on a clear day like today the hotel had far-reaching views over the ocean. How Ellie used to love to sit on the seat her dad had made her under the window and watch the big ships on the horizon, trying to guess what country they were heading for, and dreaming of sailing off to see the world herself one day. Ellie's room was just as she left it when she'd moved out six years ago. Mum cleaned it, of course, and put fresh bedding on every time Ellie came to stay but the contents remained untouched. The soft toys from Ellie's childhood sat on a shelf across the far wall, her shell collection still cluttered the windowsill and her dreamcatcher fluttered at the window. The only things she'd taken with her were her clothes and laptop. Gradually she'd started to leave a basic collection of clothes, jeans, tee shirts, summer dresses, jumpers and underwear in the wardrobe for emergency supplies if she came down and stayed longer than she intended.

She walked over to the window and looked out over the rooftops at the harbour, flanked on one side by huge cliffs where a smattering of whitewashed houses nestled. A couple of colourful boats were moored next to the jetty, swaying slightly on the rippling sea. Alongside it was the soft golden sands of the town beach, popular with holidaymakers and tourists who just wanted a quick paddle, or half hour in the sun. Opening the window, she leaned out and inhaled the salty sea air. It was good to be home. She loved Cornwall. Always had from the moment they had moved down here when she was six years old. She probably would never have left if it hadn't been for Lee. Lee and Zoe. The two people she had been closest to, trusted. Her two best friends. So she'd thought.

She shrugged. That was years ago. History. She'd moved on since then made a new life for herself. One that she enjoyed.

She showered, changed into a cool lemon cotton dress, tied her long, chestnut brown hair off her face, replaced her prescription sunglasses with contact lenses then went down to the kitchen to make herself a much needed coffee and sandwich. Exactly half an hour later she joined Mandy at the reception desk, taking her unfinished coffee with her. "Thanks for holding the fort, Mandy. I owe you one. Come in a bit later in the morning to make up for the extra time you've worked."

The older woman shook her head. "I will not. You need all the help you can get while Sue's ill. I'll be in for the first shift." She pointed to the notebook. "I've left you a couple of messages and the bookings are all up to date but phone me if you need me. Anytime."

"Thank you. I will. Now go home!" Ellie told her firmly.

Mandy grabbed her bag. "I'm out of here. It's all yours."

Ellie placed her coffee on the shelf, away from the computer, and sat on the comfy red swivel chair. She selected the admin file and entered the password - knowing that Mum always kept to the same one because she was scared of forgetting it - anxious to check the books and find out how the hotel was doing. She'd already clocked that the curtains and cushion covers in the foyer looked faded and the windows needed a clean. Not at all like her mum who always prided herself on keeping Gwel Teg immaculate. That, and the reduction in staff was triggering alarm bells in Ellie's mind.

"Excuse me."

The man's voice made her jolt. Ellie tore her eyes away from the figures on the computer screen and looked up, straight into a pair of deep grey eyes set in a ruggedly handsome face topped by chocolate-brown hair. *Very nice.* It took her a few seconds to realise that it was Merc Guy, now wearing a black tee shirt and jeans, and to notice the angry set of his jaw and the frown lines in the middle of his thick eyebrows. He was staying here then. Great. An unhappy customer was all she needed. She just hoped he didn't recognise her from this afternoon when he was blasting his horn at her. Thank goodness she'd been wearing sunglasses.

She fixed a pleasant smile on her face. "Can I help you?"

"The shower isn't working in my room and I have an important business meeting in less than an hour," he informed her curtly. "So will you either arrange for it to be fixed immediately or provide me with the use of a shower in another room?"

Great. Problems already.

"Did you hear what I said? I haven't time to waste. I have an important meeting to go to."

The man's abrupt tone annoyed her but she kept calm. "Of course, Mr...er..." she glanced at the hotel register for the man's name.

"Mitchell." He supplied. "Reece Mitchell. I arrived

earlier today. And I'm in a hurry."

Yes, I got that. A quick glance at the register told her that Reece Mitchell was in Room 12. Luckily the room next to him was empty and there was a connecting door between the rooms. Problem solved.

"I do apologise, Mr Mitchell. I'll get it sorted for you today. Meanwhile, please use the shower in the room next to you. It's vacant at the moment and you can access it through a connecting door." She reached for the key and handed it to him. "I'm very sorry for the inconvenience. Would you mind popping the key back on your way out?"

He didn't look too pleased. "Well, I guess it will have to do. I must say this hotel isn't what I'd expected. I'm surprised you do any business at all." He almost snatched the key out of her hand.

She swallowed the angry retort that sprung to her mouth reminding herself of Mum's mantra that the customer was always right. And if they weren't you didn't tell them so. She watched, fuming, as Reece Mitchell stormed off.

What an arrogant man!

Chapter Two

Reece Mitchell was right though, Ellie acknowledged. Gwel Teg was in a state and there were hardly any staff. Her mother seemed to have cut things right down to the bone, which wasn't surprising as even though Ellie had only had time to glance at the figures she could see that the hotel was hardly making any profit at all. Mum was obviously struggling to manage since Dad had died two years ago.

She bit her lip as memories of the night she'd received the late night phone call informing her that her Dad had died flooded back.

"Ellie, I am so sorry lovey. It's your Dad." Mandy's voice was breaking and Ellie's stomach clenched as she instinctively knew what was coming next. The tears spilled out of her eyes as she listened to Mandy's words. 'They did everything they could, love.'

Mandy had assured Ellie that his death was instant and he wouldn't have suffered at all. She was trying her best to comfort her but Ellie was devastated to think she would never see her lovely, kind, dependable dad again. He'd always been there to turn to and offer advice – sometimes advice she didn't ask for, Ellie remembered with a smile. She had immediately packed a bag and driven down to Cornwall, knowing how heartbroken her mum would be. Her parents had been together for forty years, they were childhood sweethearts. They loved running Gwel Teg together. Mum dealt with all the admin and looked after the guests while Dad did all the maintenance, made sure everything was in working order – and entertained the guests at the bar in the evening with jokes and anecdotes. How would Mum manage without him?

Ellie had taken compassionate leave from work and spent a few weeks helping out until Sue had shooed her back home insisting she could cope just fine. And continued insisting that she was managing perfectly well, in their twice weekly chats.

I shouldn't have taken Mum's word for it. I should have visited more often. Then she wouldn't have ended up making herself ill.

Guilt flooded through her. She was an only child, all the close family her mother had, yet had been too too wrapped up in her own life to spare any time for her mum.

A key flung down on the counter in front of her startled her back to the present.

"Well, I've managed but that bloody shower's leaking! I'm not impressed with the standard here at all."

It was Reece Mitchell again. And what a transformation. The tee shirt and jeans had been replaced by a snazzy black suit that fitted so well it just had to be designer. Teamed with a navy and white pin-striped shirt and a navy tie he really looked something. And far too important to be staying in a sleepy little seaside town like Port Medden.

Stop gawping every time you see him!

She pulled herself together. "I'm so sorry. I'll arrange for both showers to be fixed..." she started to say but he was already walking briskly away. *God he was so rude!* She hoped none of the other guests were as unpleasant.

She reached for the phone, dialled Harry's number and asked him to come and take a look at the showers in Room 12 and 13. "Can you do it asap, please?" she asked. "The guest is a real grouch."

"Of course, Miss Truman."

Ellie smiled, the old man had worked at the hotel for years but still insisted on calling Ellie Miss Truman and her mother Mrs Truman, despite them constantly telling him to drop these formalities. He was one of the old school and nothing would ever change him.

"Thank you, Harry. I'm going to have a look around in the morning and make a list of any repairs that need doing. Could you see to them all before my mother comes out of hospital? I'd like to get the place as straight as possible for her."

"Of course. I did tell your mother about a few jobs that needed doing but..." he paused, as if he feared he might be overstepping the mark.

"Go on, please," she urged him.

"Well, between me and you I think things are a bit difficult for Mrs Truman right now, money-wise I mean."

Ellie had suspected as much. "I see. Well if you let me know what the jobs are and the approximate cost I'll see what I can do."

"Certainly, Miss Truman. And how is your mother?"

"Recovering well, thank you, but she'll be in hospital a few more days." *And she'll be back in again if she doesn't take it easy. I've got to find a way to help her.*

Ellie spent the rest of the evening trying to sort out the figures. She was shocked to discover that the hotel was running at a loss and had been for the past few months. Why hadn't Mum mentioned it to her? Probably because she didn't want to worry her. Well now Ellie knew and she *was* worried.

The day had started off wrong and carried on that way, Reece thought as he walked into the foyer of Gwel Teg later that evening. He'd been stuck in traffic on the way down from London, the quaint hotel his secretary had booked him into at very short notice had turned out to be a small shabby family one run on a skeleton staff. The shower in his room wasn't working and to top it all the deal he'd been hoping to complete today had fallen through. All in all a wasted trip. Steve, his business partner, had warned him that Adam Hobson was having second thoughts though but Reece had been hoping to talk him round.

He and Steve both agreed that they wanted another business in the South West though which meant Reece would have to remain in Cornwall for a few more days and find a replacement. Not at this hotel though. Tomorrow he'd find somewhere a bit more upmarket.

He glanced over and saw that the receptionist was still hard at work on the computer. He watched her for a minute, biting her lip and frowning as she stared at the screen. She was pretty – beautiful, actually – with hazel almond shaped eyes, a tumbling cascade of rich brown hair which she'd now released from the band that constrained it, high cheekbones and perfect cupid bow lips. She looked tired, he noticed. And worried. He shouldn't have been so hard on her this afternoon. It wasn't her fault the shower wasn't working. Although her holding him up at the traffic lights earlier and then nearly driving into him as he came out of the car park to go to his pre-meeting brief with Steve hadn't helped his mood when he was already late. Still, he wasn't normally so bad-tempered, he should make amends. He paused, then walked over to the desk.

"Still working then?" He smiled, to show her that he wasn't always so cranky.

She looked up, startled. "Mr Mitchell. Is everything all right? I believe that your shower's been fixed now, although I haven't had time to check yet." She obviously thought he'd come to complain again.

"That's good. Thank you." He flashed her what he knew was a devastating smile. It never failed to win anyone over. "Look, sorry if I was a bit of a grouch this afternoon – and for blasting my horn at you earlier. Twice," he added ruefully. "I had an important meeting to go to."

She blinked and stared at him as if momentarily stunned. Damn, had he been that much of a grouch? Then her cheeks bunched endearingly as she smiled back. "And you could do without the shower not working? I guess that me holding you up earlier and cutting you up in the car park, didn't help either. I was a bit…distracted. Sorry."

"Apology accepted." For a moment their eyes locked and he felt an irresistible tug. He drew in his breath. She was pretty hot but making out with the receptionist wasn't his style. "Well, I'm off to bed now. Night."

"Night."

He walked away then glanced back but she'd already returned her attention to the computer screen. It was almost midnight now, surely she wasn't on duty all night? Was the hotel really so short staffed? No wonder it looked so in need of repair.

As he stepped into the lift it suddenly occurred to him that this hotel might be just he was looking for. It was in a great position with fantastic views, there was plenty of potential for improvement, and it was obvious that the owner was struggling with its upkeep so might be happy to sell for a knockdown price. Maybe he wouldn't check out tomorrow as he'd planned

Chapter Three

The high-pitched squawk of the seagulls jerked Ellie out of a deep sleep. It took her a couple of seconds to realise where she was then she bounded out of bed and over to the window, pulling open the curtains. What a glorious day. She gazed out in delight at the sun sparkling on the cobalt ocean just a few minutes away, positively begging her to walk barefoot over the golden sand and paddle in the cool sea.

What was stopping her? Mandy had insisted on covering the morning shift so she could spare half an hour to walk down to the beach, surely? The fresh sea air would do her good.

Ellie remembered her dad always telling her, 'make time to enjoy life.' It was a mantra she often repeated to herself. She enjoyed her work as a PR officer helping firms improve their image by 'giving back to society' but spending her childhood in Cornwall had taught her that taking time out, relaxing with family and friends, doing things you enjoyed were just as important.

Whenever she visited her parents her first stop, often before catching up on their news, was the beach.

She showered and pulled on a pair of electric blue shorts and a white vest top over lacy white underwear. Ever since the total mortification of being examined by a very dishy doctor while attired in greying underwear after she'd slipped over in Ben's Bistro two years ago, hurting her bum and ending up in A&E, Ellie always wore pretty, matching underwear. She grabbed a bottle of sun lotion from her dressing table and rubbed some sun cream onto her exposed limbs and neck.

"Did you sleep well, lovey?" Mandy asked as Ellie walked into the foyer.

"I flaked out as soon as my head hit the pillow. I think I must have been shattered. Are you okay to look after thing here while I have a walk along the beach? I'll only be half an hour or so."

"No problem. Take as much time as you want. I doubt if we'll be very busy." Mandy switched to the booking screen. "We've got a couple of guests leaving today. Mr Mitchell from Room 12 and Mr and Mrs Wilson from Room 4."

So Merc Guy was leaving. Good, she didn't want another run in with him. Mind you, he'd been nice last night. She'd been surprised when he'd apologised. He'd actually seemed rather charming. She guessed his meeting had gone well so he'd been in a better mood. In her experience, many business men were like that, they switched on the charm when it suited them and switched it off just as easily.

"Have we got any other guests booked in?" she asked. When she checked the register last night there were only seven and if three were leaving...

"There's a Mr and Mrs Smythe booking in tomorrow but that's all for the foreseeable."

June and the hotel wasn't even half full. Ellie remembered when Gwel Teg was teeming in the summer months, her parents often had to turn people away.

"How long are the Smythes staying for?" she asked.

Mandy glanced at the computer screen. "Two nights. They've asked for the Honeymoon suite. Apparently they spent their honeymoon here and now it's their Silver Wedding Anniversary so they want the same room."

"How romantic." Ellie paused." Maybe I should check out the room before I go for a walk. Mr Mitchell's shower was out of order yesterday and the one in the connecting room was leaking, he got in a real strop about it. I don't want any other guests upset."

"Don't worry, I checked the room yesterday afternoon and it's all fine." Mandy glanced at her. "So you've met Mr Mitchell yet? Quite a hunk isn't he?"

Ellie shrugged. "Is he? I hadn't noticed."

"Course you haven't, lovey." Mandy gave her a knowing wink.

Ellie ignored her and continued. "I was looking through the books last night. Things aren't going well, are they?"

"They'll pick up again. The hotel needs a bit of TLC and your mum hasn't been up to it but she'll get her mojo back, you'll see. Now be off with you. Go take that walk!" Mandy shooed her away.

I hope Mandy's right and things do pick up again, Ellie thought as she set off down the hill towards the beach. Mum wasn't getting any younger. She was in her sixties now and should be thinking about retiring and taking it easy, not struggling to run a small hotel. It was a lot of work for her. Perhaps Ellie could persuade her to think about selling up and buying a little bungalow instead.

Property was expensive in Port Medden, as in any part of Cornwall. Would there be enough left from the proceeds of the hotel to allow Mum to purchase a bungalow, and have enough to live on until she received her pension? Ellie bit her lip. She doubted it. Not unless she moved away, perhaps up to the Midlands nearer to Ellie.

No, that wouldn't work. Mum loved Cornwall. She would hate to live somewhere else.

Reaching the wall that overlooked the beach, Ellie looked over at the golden sand and glistening, almost turquoise, ocean and saw that there were already a few holidaymakers taking advantage of the low tide to paddle. A family with two children were building a sandcastle near the shore and a pair of teenage lovers were walking along the water's edge, holding hands and laughing as the sea lapped over their bare feet.

Just like she and Lee had done.

The memories were still there but six years had passed and the pain had long since gone. At first, it was all so raw that Ellie had avoided coming down to visit her parents. Soon though she had made a new life, new friends and was so busy she hardly ever thought of Lee but it had taken her a year to bring herself to come down to Port Medden again. Her parents had been delighted to see her, although had never reproached her for staying away.

After a while, Lee and Zoe moved to Bristol so Ellie no longer had to worry about bumping into them. Her parents were careful not to mention them when Ellie visited but she heard that they got married, had a couple of children.

She was glad now that Lee had finished with her, even if it was because he had fallen in love with her best friend. If he hadn't cheated on her they would probably be married now and it would be Ellie who was tied down with a couple of kids, never having had chance to find out who she was and what she wanted. She'd seen it happen to so many people. They met someone, fell in love and before you could blink had forgotten all about the plans they'd made for their future, their dreams, friends, the things they liked doing. They became 'a couple' and it was as if they stopped existing as a single unit. Everything had to be done together.

Well that wasn't for her. Not that she had massive plans for the future, she was enjoying her job, taking each day as it came. No one to answer to or to have to think about. Yes, she had dates. Lots of them. Kate, her best friend, laughingly called Ellie a 'serial dater' because she didn't allow any relationship to get serious, never went out with anyone for longer than a couple of months. That way the relationship kept its freshness and they both parted with good memories.

And it made sure she never got hurt again.

She walked down the steps then slipped off her sandals, relishing the feel of the soft sand beneath her bare feet as she ran over to the sea. She paddled for a while, letting the cool water lap over her feet. She'd always found the sea soothing. Many a time as a troubled teenager she'd sat on this beach, staring out at the ocean, marvelling at the vastness and wildness of it all. Whatever had been bothering her had faded away into insignificance and she'd always walked back home feeling lighter, as if she'd got things into perspective.

She remembered how she'd sat here for hours that day before she left, wondering if she was making the right decision. Was she letting Zoe and Lee drive her away? By the time she'd walked off the beach Ellie had been confident that she was doing the right thing. She needed a fresh start. To make a new life for herself. And it had been a good decision. She loved her life in the city and her job but that didn't stop her feeling guilty about leaving her mum to manage on her own these past two years.

Her mobile pinged in her bag. She reached for it and glanced at the screen. Kate.

Hows ur mum, hun?

She'd answered Kate's advert for a flat share when she'd decided to move up to the Midlands, thinking it would do while she sorted herself out. They'd hit it off straight away and Ellie had remained there.

Weak but ok. She'll be in for a few days yet. How r u?

They exchanged messages for a while then Ellie set off back up the hill, past the pretty, quaint tea rooms, the bakery and souvenir shop, until the charming white hotel came into sight. She paused for a moment to look at it, as a potential guest would, taking in the slightly neglected but still colourful hanging baskets and plant tubs that adorned the outside. Okay, the outside could do with a coat of paint and it needed some repairs but it was full of character and the location was stunning. She was determined to get Gwel Teg back into shape before Mum came out of hospital. And first stop was to check all the rooms and see what repairs needed doing. She didn't want to give any of the other guests cause to complain. Bad reviews on TripAdvisor wouldn't help gain more bookings.

Mandy wasn't at the reception desk. Guessing she'd gone for a loo break, Ellie picked up a notebook and the set of master keys. As it was a sunny day she imagined that their guests would probably be out so she should be able to check all the rooms before the cleaners did their rounds.

She made her way around the first floor, most of the rooms were unoccupied. Before she entered the ones that were occupied, she checked that the 'Do Not Disturb' label wasn't on the door then knocked loudly and called out before entering. Careful not to touch anything personal, she noted any repairs that needed doing. There were quite a few but they were mostly minor things that Harry could tackle. She was dismayed to see how dated and shabby the rooms looked though.

It looks like the whole hotel needs refurbishing, she thought as she made her way to the second floor.

She hesitated outside Room 12. Had Reece Mitchell left yet? She really didn't want another run-in with him. He might have been pleasant last night but her first impressions of him weren't good and she definitely didn't want a repeat performance.

She glanced at her watch. 10.45. Guests had to vacate the rooms by ten so he should be long gone. Even so, she banged on the door and listened intently just to be sure. Nope, there was no sound coming from the room. She unlocked the door and stepped inside.

Glancing around, she immediately spotted that a couple of drawer handles were missing on the bedside cabinet, a plug socket was loose and the carpet was threadbare in one corner. *Not good. It's a wonder he hadn't complained about that.*

She made a note of them and starred them as urgent. She'd ask Harry to do them this afternoon, at least they wouldn't cost anything. And perhaps she could find a small cupboard to put over the threadbare patch of carpet.

She looked over at the closed ensuite door. She'd better check the shower too, and the one in the connecting room. Best to make sure they'd both been fixed before she booked anyone else into the room.

As she walked over to the ensuite the door handle turned. She stared at it, horrified. *Oh heck - he wasn't?*

The door started to open.

She'd better get out of here. Fast.

But before she could move the door was thrust open and Reece Mitchell walked out, completely naked, rubbing his hair with a towel.

Available in paperback and eBook formats

For more information about **Karen King**

and other **Accent Press** titles

please visit

www.accentpress.co.uk

Printed in Great Britain
by Amazon